DANIEL
BRASS
LEGIONNAIRE

ACKNOWLEDGMENTS

THE STORY YOU ARE ABOUT to read started as an inside joke. For some reason, it just wouldn't leave me alone. I spent an entire summer and fall typing, fiddling, and reworking Brass Legionnaire. In many ways, it reflects things I love to see and peruse about in my own reading. Action, adventure, sacrifice, growth, love, pain, and despair – all have their place in the story. Before I let you read, there are a few people I'd like to thank. To my parents and family, thanks for supporting me and always having my back. To my Aunt Susan Ottalini, your generosity won't be forgotten. To Tabatha and Glendon Haddix over at Streetlight Graphics, you guys made the world of Imperial Rome more alive than I ever could. To my editor, Marg Gilks at Scriptora Editing Services, my book would suck without you (Not stealing from a song at all!). To my friends who provided hours of beta reading – Emma, Allison, Alyssa, and all the others who contributed in one way or another, thanks for catching my little blunders. To Chris Valentine, thanks for the super awesome bonus artwork for the website. Thanks to my Kickstarter pals – John Idlor, Stefan Vilpula, Stephen Meyer, Daniel Winterhalter, Lindsay Buroker, Maria Grenchik, Rel ná DecVandé, M.C.A. Hogarth, Alexander, and all the others for helping take the pain out of editing and publishing on a teacher's salary. To my brother Russell, who reliably informs me that Constantine 'sounds a bit like an obnoxious snob until you get to know him' thanks for being the voice of Constantine and all the others.

Finally, to my dearest Eduarda, you made the inside joke come to life and pushed me to do my best. Thanks for putting up with my 'twenty cool facts about the book' talks and the endless supply of steampunky related blabber. This book wouldn't have been finished without you.

Daniel Ottalini
April, 2012

The Imperial Roman Empire around the time of the Brittenburg Incident.

A brief view of the majestic, industrial metropolis of Brittenburg, the jewel of Germania Inferior.

CHAPTER

1

ORKING HIS WRENCH WITH THE deftness of long experience, Julius Brutus Caesar tightened the bolt on the exposed sprocket. When it was connected to the rest of the engine, the engineers could begin the final assembly of yet another mechaniphant. Not for the first time, Julius wondered why on earth someone had wanted to invent such a mechanical monstrosity in the first place. Although it was impressive, he had to admit. Standing over fifteen imperial feet tall, with a protected driver's seat and razor-sharp chain tusks, it was perfect for crashing through the center of an enemy's battle line, especially when combined with other mechaniphants in a thunderous charge.

Julius shook his head to clear his wandering mind and studied his work in the light from the gas lanterns burning all around the factory. He wiped a sheen of sweat from his forehead with the back of his hand, product of his exertion despite the large open windows far above his head, just below the steam pipes haphazardly crisscrossing near the ceiling amidst spindly gantries and support struts. The whole factory was a safety inspector's nightmare, but of course the inspector had been bribed, so the whole situation was swept under the rug, so to speak.

Much better, he thought as he carefully cleaned his wrench with a dirty rag pulled from a pouch on his utility belt. A loud whistle blast signaled the end of the work day. Tucking the rag back into his belt, Julius trudged across the factory floor toward the massive steel doors, their paint peeling around splotches of rust. The air smelled of bitter industrial coolants, welding smoke, and various other chemicals despite the fresh air that carried the sounds and smells of Brittenburg through the windows overhead. Julius nodded greetings to several other workers as they all moved toward the pay office. Being Friday, it was payday. He hoped the overtime he'd been working would make a difference this period.

Julius's father had been injured several years ago in the same factory, when part of a mechaniphant collapsed during construction. Marcus Caesar had required hospitalization as well as a complete leg replacement. The medical bills continued to pile up, and it was all Julius could do, as the main family breadwinner now, to stave off eviction from their small Sludge Bottom apartment. With three other family members to support, Julius had thrown himself into his job at the factory, hoping to impress his supervisors enough to be promoted and get a raise.

The workers quietly queued up before the office window, waiting while the paymaster checked his charts and notes before grudgingly handing over a small handful of copper and silver coins to each worker. "Caesar, Julius B.," Julius told the attendant as he stepped up to the window.

"Here you go, Julius, and don't bother counting; I added in what you earned in overtime. So no complaining!" The paymaster's gruff rumble contrasted with his thin, weedy appearance. His lips, nearly concealed by a thin, droopy mustache, barely moved as he talked.

Ignoring him, Julius did a quick count of the coins. "That's all?" he asked incredulously. It was barely more than he had earned in the last period. "I was here for thirty extra hours this week!"

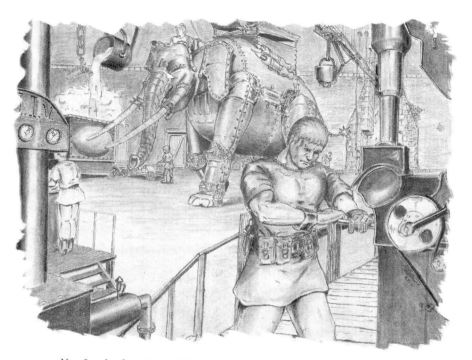

Not for the first time, Julius wondered why on earth someone had wanted to invent such a mechanical monstrosity in the first place.

"Oh, yeah?" the older man sneered. "Well, money don't grow on trees, you know. Since you're our resident emperor, how about you just command money to appear? Ha! Ha-ha-ha!" He doubled over, his laughter ending in a wheezing cough.

Julius glared. "You're a real Plato, aren't you?" he mumbled as he scooped up his denarii and walked through the steel factory doors into the murky sunlight of a Brittenburg afternoon, once again cursing his family for naming him after the founder of the empire.

Outside, the cobblestone streets of Brittenburg, otherwise known as Majoris Brittenburgia, factory city and capital of the Imperial Roman Province of Germania Inferior, were filled with people, machines, and animals. Julius navigated past booksellers, out-of-town merchants, a pair of barbarians with matching trousers and face tattoos standing next to an aviator in a long leather flying jacket, goggles hanging around his neck, and a group of school children being herded along by a matronly woman and a portly teacher. Julius's home was on the west side of town, almost right against the massive curtain wall that was both defensive fortification and bay dike. The area was dark, dank, and affectionately known as Sludge Bottom to the rest of the city.

On a whim, Julius stepped over the electrified rails of the motortrollies and entered a bakery, the opening door triggering a mechanical bird in the corner to squawk, "Customer! Customer!"

An older woman wearing a smock over her gray dress walked out of the back. Recognizing him, she waved a greeting. "Hello, Julius! Picking up groceries for the family?"

"Naw, just grabbing a snack." He looked carefully through the clouded glass display windows. "Are those honey nut tarts?" he asked excitedly. The heavily glazed treats were a traditional Brittenburg desert and snack food, popular with everyone from the lowest plebeian to the governor himself, who was rumored to have devoured trays of them on his own.

"Absolutely! You know how hard they are to keep in stock. Ignacious is starting another batch to make sure we have enough for tomorrow." She handed him the usual loaf of bread with one hand and a small, delicate box with the other. "Take the runt of the batch for free; it will go stale, otherwise. And make sure your sister gets at least a bite!" she shouted at him as his smile went from overjoyed to smirk in a heartbeat.

"Crumbs count as a bite, don't they?" he quipped as he paid for the loaf of bread. It was still warm and he wrapped it in paper against the chill in the air. Fall was coming to the city, and with it, the rainy season that made living in Brittenburg all the more challenging.

A horn called nearby as he paused at a street corner to tear off a chunk of bread, and he found himself wandering closer to see what the fuss was about.

A short, stocky man with an amplification device stood on a raised platform, haranguing the crowd. "Patricians and plebeians, servants and republicans, my countrymen! The Imperial Army is recruiting! We have need of good, strapping young men to join the newest, most extraordinary legion, the XIII Germania! The Imperial Senate clamors for war. Will you join your countrymen to bring punishment and pain to the barbarians and bloodthirsty raiders, those dastardly pillagers and savages who steal children, destroy livelihoods, enslave our women, and kill our men? Will you join with me?" His voice echoed around the square.

The crowd cheered. A throng of young men rushed toward the clouds of steam that marked the location of waiting wagons, eager to enlist. Although the Empire had long ago eliminated compulsory military service for all male citizens, many families continued to see military service as a constant, required duty. The military paid well and consistently, no small feat for an empire stretching over half the known world.

For a moment Julius considered enlisting. He was the right age and in great shape, both mentally and physically, but he doubted his ability to complete the training necessary to earn a place as a legionary in the Imperial Legions. Instead he watched as, one by one, men were led into a steam wagon where, presumably, they would be examined to see if they were fit for duty. He didn't realize he'd walked closer until the recruiting legionnaire was suddenly right in front of him.

"Good day, son; looking for a little excitement and a chance to see the world?" the man asked, his tone chipper.

Julius considered. Although that did sound fun, he had more practical things to worry about. "I'd love to, but I've got to take care of my family here."

The legionary smiled knowingly and scanned Julius top to toe with his eyes. Apparently Julius passed muster, because he said, "Do you know about the signing bonus? And the monthly paychecks? We can have them deposited straight to your bank account here. If your parents have telecom service, you can even hear them over the wireless when you're at base."

Julius was intrigued. "How much is the signing bonus?"

The legionnaire named a figure. Julius felt his eyebrows rise.

"I can tell you need some time to think about it. But don't take too long, and miss out on this chance. The army offers mobility, a chance to improve your life. Don't stay here and be a slave, a cog in some factory for the rest of your life. That's not much to tell your grandkids about."

The recruiter's eyes met Julius's, eyes that had seen way too much in this world. "I wouldn't trade my experiences for anything," he said in a softer voice, as if he had read Julius's mind. Then his tone grew brisk. "We'll be here for three more days. Simply ask for us at the auxilia barracks. After that we march for Camp Titus, near the Black Forest. You get the signing bonus the moment you sign on the dotted line and receive the tin *Aquila,* the symbol of legionnaires in training. I'm Duplicarius Apollonius, head recruiter." The soldier held out his hand. Julius extended his own, and after giving it a firm shake, Apollonius moved off into the crowd.

Julius resumed his walk home, his heart beating a little faster as he envisioned himself proudly wearing the uniform of the legion. His only worry was how he would convince his parents.

~ * * * ~

Marcus Caesar's calloused fist slammed onto the scuffed dinner table. "*No.* No, no, no. No son of mine is going to join the legions. You are this"—he held up his thumb and forefinger, their tips nearly touching—"close to getting that promotion. I can feel it in my bones. Even my metal ones." He slapped his brass replacement leg, which responded with a hollow reverberation.

Julius held his father's stare from across the table. A few years ago, he would not have been able to maintain that stare for long. Now, his father's brown eyes reflected how living in one of the poorest areas of the city had drained him, both mentally and physically. The past few years had deepened the lines on his face and peppered his curly black hair with gray.

Marcus cracked a nut in his hand and popped it into his mouth. "Aurelia, give me a hand here."

"Now, Marcus," Aurelia Marcia said softly from her place before the sink, washing dishes. They were now unable to pay for household help, so Julius's mother did most of the chores. Her slender, fine-boned hands wiped the dishrag over the dirty plates and whirled it within the cups. "He's old enough to make his own decisions. I don't want him joining the legions either, but we're at peace. You know a peacetime army does little more than march in circles and look nice for the praetors."

Marcus scowled and turned back to Julius. "I am still the *paterfamilias* of this household and I say you will not be joining the legions!"

Julius had never heard his father yell before. He preferred to convince his children to follow a certain path, rather than simply demand that they follow his will.

The floorboards creaked and Julius heard the pitter-patter of small feet just before seven-year-old Marciena entered the room. "Momma, why is Papa yelling?" she asked, her brown curls jostling one another as she moved to press herself to her mother's side like a thin shadow.

Aurelia gave her husband a tired look as she dried her hands on her apron. She placed the last of the dishes in the autodryer, turned the crank, and walked away as the machine began to emit a low-pitched whine.

Marcus pushed his chair back and stood, leaning heavily on his cane. His mechanical leg squealed and hissed, finally settling into the groove of walking as his leg bent and flexed at the knee joint. He walked over to the autodryer and smacked it on its side. "Holy Emperor, this stupid piece of scrap metal never seems to work." He smacked it again for good measure and the machine's whine faded to a low, steady hum. "I'm amazed it's stayed together this long. Gonna have to break out the wrench-spanner tomorrow and take this thing apart to see where that wire's crossed." He turned to look at Julius. "You'll help me, right?" It sounded like a plea.

Julius mustered his courage. "Father, I know it's been hard for us, but this is our way out. The army pays better than the factory does. They also offer a signing bonus—twenty-five denarii! That will pay off our loans and you'll own this place. I'll even have my pay sent back here, so Marciena can go to school and you and Momma won't have to worry." He set his mug down on the table. His fingers felt the cracks in the mug, repaired again and again by his mother to stretch every coin they had. "We need the money. It's the only thing we can do."

His father was staring out the window over the kitchen sink, gazing at the reflections from the gas lights sparkling in the glass windows of the city. A steamwagon clattered and chugged along the street below, metal wheels grinding against the pavement. "Looks like fog tonight," he observed, his voice a low rumble. He turned to glance at his only son, who shifted on the three-legged stool at the table.

I wonder what he is seeing, Julius thought, noting the distant, almost glazed look in the old man's eyes.

With a small jerk of his head, Marcus brought his attention back to the present. "You cannot leave. You do not have my blessing." Emotion choked his voice.

Julius sighed as his father stumped out of the room. While he had known it would be a challenge to bring his father around, he hadn't anticipated such extreme opposition. He had hoped his father would support him.

His mother walked back into the kitchen. She put her arm around his shoulder and gave it a tight squeeze. Possessed of a gentle soul, she rarely expressed anger or frustration. Aurelia was similar to the clothing she wove and sold to the poor people of the slums: simple and plain, but tough and strong, too. Not flashy or rich, but dependable and long-lasting. His mother had made a life for herself, here in the slums.

She sat down next to Julius. "Your father is not angry at you. He's angry that you are leaving your family. You have responsibilities here—to your community, to the factory, and to your sister and father and me." Her voice had fallen almost to a whisper, blending with the sounds of the city that crept into the quiet kitchen: the clanking and whirring of a walker patrolling nearby; the occasional screech of metal against rusted metal; the faint crash of waves against the city wall behind them.

"Can you bring Papa around? I have to go. This is about my only chance to get out of here, to see the Empire. Can you imagine, Mother? There is a world beyond these black iron walls, beyond this stinking slum. I can't stay here. I'll leave without his blessing, if I have to."

She smiled wanly. "Sometimes I think it's hard for your father to see how much of him there is in you. I'll do my best to bring him around. You know how he needs time to adjust. Now, you get some sleep. We'll discuss this further in the morning." She rose and moved quietly from the room.

Julius gathered his thoughts and left the kitchen, the gears in his head turning full tilt. As he lay in his bed, close to falling asleep, he heard the susurration of his mother's whispered prayers to the gods for his safety. Her voice lulled him to sleep.

~ * * * ~

A few blocks away, the constabulary auxilia walker *Maxentius III* slogged its way through the darkened streets of Sludge Bottom, traditionally not a bastion of law and order in the vibrant mechanical city of Brittenburg. Under pressure from various city council members, merchants, and the provincial senators, the governor had agreed to send in patrols both day and night. The constable auxiliary forces were, understandably, not pleased by this turn of events. After all, they reasoned, the auxiliaries were the ones putting their necks on the line in old and jury-rigged equipment, not the governor or his flunkies.

The four-man patrol were stationed at various points on the flat-topped walker as its four legs moved it like a giant beetle through the streets. The vehicle was about ten feet tall, with the low railing fortified into "nests" at the front and rear; the under-officer in charge of the patrol stood in the nest in the front tip, the best vantage point on the machine. A lantern just below the horn-like gantry illuminated the area in front of the walker, and several searchlights swept back and forth, running off power supplied by the clanking steam engine.

Moving through Sludge Bottom was always risky late at night, so they had both running lights and security lights on, temporarily brightening the narrow alleyways and side streets, washing over piles of debris and catching the furtive movements of scurrying rats and *larger* things in the darkness.

An odd feeling tingled over the weathered skin at the back of the under-officer's neck. Twenty years of constabulary instinct were telling him that something was not right. The streets shouldn't be quite this silent, especially in the Sludge Bottom quarter. Where were the bar patrons? The loitering drunks, the rabble, the downtrodden masses? It was still early into the evening watch. So where were the people?

Clattering on the shingles of a nearby building caught his attention. He turned toward the sound, one hand reaching for the control panel in front of him to swing the front searchlight up at the dark roof on his right. The blazing light caught a flurry of movement, then nothing.

The under-officer turned to the other auxiliaries in his patrol. The constable manning the rear post, watching behind the patrol, had also turned toward the noise on the roof. The helmsman and wireless operator, seated at their controls under a small canvas canopy rigged in the middle of the flat deck, remained focused on their jobs. They seemed ignorant of the sudden unease that permeated the soupy air.

He scanned the rooftops. A shadow poked out from behind a chimney. Throwing his arm up to point at the figure, the under-officer called, "You there! Identify—"

A crossbow bolt tore through his neck, sending him over the railing circling the top of the walker. Spraying blood trailed him through the air, spattering the walker's rust-streaked side as he tumbled toward the cobblestones below. He landed with a sickening thud and lay still.

At this point the helmsman made a grave error. Instead of continuing on at full speed to escape the ambush, his hands left the controls of the walker to reach for his weapons. The walker lurched to a stop, one leg raised precariously a foot or so off the ground. The auxiliary next to him looked surprised, and the helmsman smacked him on the head. "Quick, boy, get a message off that we are under attack!" If the operator could get a message off, help would arrive quickly.

The last member of the patrol was fighting for his life against a cloaked figure that had jumped from the slate roof onto the walker. He'd lifted his *spatha* in time to block the first blow, but subsequent thrusts of the cloaked figure's twin daggers pushed him back toward the center of the walker. The half-trained constable could do little more than parry and retreat again and again, his boots clanking along the gantry until his foot caught on a protruding screw and he stumbled. His sword wavered for a moment as he instinctively turned his head to look behind him.

That one moment was all the shadowy figure needed. Silver flashed in the security lights as a dagger shot out, quickly jabbing into his leg, then his arm, then his neck.

Blood spurted and the luckless auxiliary slumped to the deck. With a powerful kick, the cloaked figure sent the body rolling under the railing and over the side of the gantry.

Seeing this, the helmsman drew his sword and battered shield from the rack beside him and charged. Several grappling hooks arched over the sides and fixed on the railings, and he knew it was only a matter of time until they were overrun. All he could do was stall. He slowed, keeping himself between the cloaked figure at the rear of the walker and the young auxiliary manning the radio. "Hurry! Get that signal off!" the helmsman shouted at the young operator, who sat seemingly frozen in fear.

The cloaked figure was suddenly before him, and a flurry of impacts hit his shield. The helmsman backed off, then, whirling his sword, pressed forward. For a moment, it appeared that momentum was on his side. He closed in, stabbing low.

The shadow warrior seemed to flow to one side. The helmsman's eyes widened in surprise. His sword clanged loudly off the metal decking, sparks flying. In response, the figure swept the dagger it gripped sideways into the helmsman's head, the force of the blow lifting him off his feet to fall with a thud and clank of gear to the deck plating.

The shadow figure stepped over him and approached the auxiliary at the radio, who turned around, hand grasping for the hilt of his scabbarded sword. The cloaked figure's arm snapped out, impossibly fast—

And severed the wireless radio's power cable.

The auxiliary looked up. "Hello, Mother."

The figure in the cloak nodded imperceptibly and rested a hand on his shoulder before moving away to give quiet directions to the boarders climbing from the scaling ropes over the rails. They swiftly moved to hide all evidence of their ambush while one man walked to the control console and activated the steam engines. The *Maxentius III* lurched forward.

Seeing the helmsman's chest still rising and falling, the traitorous auxiliary drew his sword and walked over to hold it over the fallen man's neck. "You never were a very good driver." He pushed the sword down.

CHAPTER

2

THE MORNING SUN DID NOT rise over Brittenburg, it oozed. Sliding over the massive black iron walls to touch the tallest chimneys and smokestacks first, it turned beige messenger doves white and blinded the wall guards manning their posts as it limned the glimmering brass towers and shining steel arches. As the sun rose higher, its light reached lower into the city, pushing through dirty panes of glass and warming clothes on wash lines.

The light worked its way down the airfield's massive wireless antennae, and slid off the ribbed canvas sides of a massive transport flyer. It glowed gold in the exhaust fumes of the cargo forklifts that idled while the transport flyer was being secured to steel posts. Gears clattered and pistons hissed as an operator jockeyed a long telescoping causeway from the squat terminal to the dirigible's passenger portal. A legionnaire stood behind him, waiting for the tube to connect to the portal.

"You guys must be born with that look," the operator said to the scowling legionnaire, who shrugged, but didn't respond. The operator turned away to carefully align the various rods and connectors that would secure the flyer's gondola to the causeway, adding, "I hope those idiotic fielders check the connection points properly this time."

At the legionnaire's quizzical look, the operator explained, "We've had more than one accident happen because some careless groundling failed to check the connection points between ship and gangway. Here by the sea, the salt air corrupts everything." The operator paused, but still got no response from the taciturn legionnaire. Turning back to his controls, he whispered a prayer to Vulcan for a successful connection as the pistons hissed and all four of the eagle seals on the causeway glowed a dull green.

The operator reached for the speaking tube. "System is set, causeway locked in place. Opening portal."

~ * * * ~

With a jet of smoke and a faint whiff of ozone, the steel door oscillated into its frame. After a moment, the passengers stepped through the portal and walked along the causeway. A waiting legionnaire scanned each face that passed his point on the corrugated metal wall where he leaned, face impassive. Constantine Tiberius Appius noted his presence as he stepped through the portal.

A fitful breeze tugged at his silk trousers and dark blue tunic and ruffled his brown hair as he paused to adjust his grip on his satchel. Then he walked up to the legionnaire and said, "Legate General Minnicus sent you?"

The soldier straightened. "Yes sir, Your Lordship, sir."

Constantine waved a tanned hand. "Don't call me that. I'm simply a tribune—just plain Tribune Appius, a simple officer, newly assigned to a new legion." He smiled, torn between amusement and relief at being able to say those words.

"Well, sir, if you don't mind me saying, we ought to get going," the older man replied, tapping his wrist chronometer. "You don't want to make a poor showing on your first day."

"And you are...?"

"Centurion Germanicus Horatitus Vibius, sir. Thirteenth Cohort, XIII Germania Legion. I'm your second in command. I've got fifteen years' experience with the III Galitica and the VII Hispana. The new legion will be based twenty-five miles northeast, at Fort Tiberius. We've been awaiting your arrival. Legion specialties include—"

Constantine cut him off. "I've read my briefing files, Centurion Vibius. I know what the legion's specialties are—or rather, what they will be." His fingers slipped under the neck of his tunic to absently fiddle with the gold medallion resting against his chest. He had found himself doing that frequently, the last few days, a nervous reaction to his first solo flight from Roma to Brittenburg via Massila along the southern coast of Gaul. Although he was "in disguise," he was certain that his parents had ensured the... *acceptability* of the other passengers and the crew, and probably had a few secret constable types hidden among them. Not that he cared; just not being waited on hand and foot by the others gave him a sense of freedom. He was sure he would get over it soon enough, but in the meantime, he was enjoying it. A chuckle escaped his lips. His older brother would have been outraged by the lack of servants, fanfare, and general respect for his position that he believed he deserved.

Centurion Vibius looked at him quizzically. "Are you ready to take command of your first cohort, sir? The last officer I worked with thought he was Augustus Caesar in the flesh. He didn't last too long. Hero types tend to get themselves—and their men—killed pretty frequently; Imperial Roman history makes that clear, sir."

Constantine understood the unasked question. The centurion was simply trying to get a feel for Constantine's thoughts about his own military prowess. He thought for a moment, crafting his reply. "Honestly, Centurion, I'm excited to be here, with the opportunity to *learn* the art of warfare from our more experienced officers. I believe I've got a few things I can bring to the table." The centurion inclined his head, accepting the answer.

"Besides, I'm sure that the legate has told you, in no uncertain terms, that if anything happens to me, there will be Hades to pay," Constantine continued, smiling at the older man.

Vibius smirked at the comment, then reached for Constantine's bag. "Are you ready to go, sir?"

"Yes, Vibius, I think it's time we left this causeway. Although the view is stunning from here, I think we ought to see more of this industrial powerhouse, don't you?"

Vibius sighed with the air of a long-suffering assistant and led the way into the terminal's bright atrium, where they were swallowed in the crowds.

Neither noticed the man wearing grubby, well-patched overalls who followed them at a distance.

~ * * * ~

The sun continued its daily ascent into the heavens. By now it was almost ten o'clock in the morning, and the light was finally reaching the lower parts of the city, piled high with tenements and apartment complexes. Julius raised a hand to shield his eyes as he walked around a corner into bright sunlight.

A high, clear horn blast echoed down the street. Pedestrians scurried out of the way as a troop of auxiliaries quick-marched past, led by an officer on an ostrichine, the mechanical walker's speakers squawking a general alarm over and over again. Its odd bobbing movements looked realistic, as far as Julius could tell. Then again, he'd never seen a real ostrich, so what did he know?

"Something must be going on," a leathery old man next to him commented.

Another passerby mentioned that a patrol had gone missing the night before. The conversation flowed around conspiracy theories, invasions by Nortlander sky pirates, and rumors of rebellions. Although Julius discounted all of those, it was rare that a fairly lawful city like Brittenburg would have a patrol disappear. There were the usual low-scale illegal activities, the occasional murder, and racketeering, prostitution, and robbery, but rarely were the actual police auxiliaries attacked. That tended to bring lots of unwelcome attention down onto *every* criminal's head. Brittenburgers were inventors and tinkerers, not murderers and rebels.

While Julius pondered this, the last pair of auxiliaries marched past, and he took advantage of the near-empty street to run most of the rest of the way to the factory.

His footsteps echoed as he walked into the building. It was oddly empty for a second shift on a Wednesday. The weedy paymaster stepped out of his office, and Julius saw a shadow in the room behind him that indicated the presence of another person. "Where is everyone?" Julius asked him. "What's going on?"

"The factory owners have declared that today is a day off," the paymaster said. "Go home and enjoy your freedom. They'll even count today as a full working day for you, so you'll get your full pay."

Julius stared at him as he digested this unexpected news. As far as he knew, the owners, whom he had never seen, had never given their workers a day off. They liked squeezing every ounce of productivity out of their employees, even at risk of their health. Even in his father's time, he doubted that there had been occasion for an unofficial day off. Well, he decided, stepping forward, now he had a chance to end his time here at the factory on a high note.

After securing his remaining pay from the paymaster, Julius informed him that he was leaving to join the army. The man's brown eyes widened and a muscle in his cheek twitched. The figure in the office behind him shifted, then settled back down.

"Well then, good luck to ya!" The paymaster shook his hand. His bones felt frail and thin within Julius's calloused grip.

Julius left him to clean out his locker. Twisting an antiquated key in the lock, he swung the door open and removed from within his utility belt, an oil-covered smock, and a small phonogadget he was building out of spare parts for Marciena. She loved playing with the odds and ends he managed to piece together into something new. He had been saving money to send her to the Brittenburg Girls' Academy, where they taught engineering and science to girls, not just needlework and cooking. *That is what a modern girl needs to know,* he thought as he regarded his handiwork on the phonogadget. *With my army paycheck, it will be far more likely that she will attend.*

He stuffed his things into his bag and turned to go, then paused as he noticed a large, canvas-covered shape at the back of the warehouse. Had third shift completed a new mechaniphant that was now awaiting transport? But no, the bulges and protrusions that would denote the contours of a standard mechaniphant were missing. *They must not have completed it entirely. It doesn't have the horns, or the enclosed driver's compartment in the front.* He frowned. *But why would it be over near the doors, rather than in the middle of the assembly line? If it isn't complete, it shouldn't have been moved.* Then he shrugged. He didn't work here anymore, so he didn't really have to care.

The warmth of the noonday sun banished any further thoughts of the mysterious, canvas-covered object from his mind as he stepped out into the bright sunlight. He grinned at the shining city around him, Germania Inferior's gear-studded jewel.

~ * * * ~

There was no sunlight on the day that Julius joined the Germania XIII Legion, only the gray smog from innumerable smokestacks that blended seamlessly with the gray clouds overhead. The warm air was motionless; even the breeze off the ocean seemed lackluster. He was one of over two thousand new recruits; another one thousand men from the surrounding towns, villages, and sub-provinces of Germania Inferior would join the legion at Fort Tiberius. Standing with his fellows in a large clump at the center of the plaza, Julius listened to the droning speeches of various bigwigs, dignitaries, and important people of the city, too bored with their self-aggrandizement and big words meant to inspire loyalty, strength, and moral fiber to be bothered by their hypocrisy.

Tuning out the latest speech, Julius turned to stare at the even larger crowd of spectators that had gathered to witness the first founding of a legion in Brittenburg's history. He spotted his little sister, sitting on his father's shoulders, and waved to her. After what seemed like an eternity, Marciena spotted him and smiled, pointing at him before waving her small arm back and forth over her head.

Her other hand clutched his goodbye gift, the phonogadget. He had recorded his voice inside it so that she could hear him even when he was away at camp. Julius had also taught her how to repair it using the tiny tool kit he had bought for her with some of his savings. *If that doesn't get her inquisitive little mind chugging away, I'm not fit to be her brother,* he thought as he returned his attention to the speakers on the platform elevated about fifty feet above the crowd.

Ceremonial horns trumpeted across the plaza. The high, clear notes silenced the low murmurs of the crowd. A tall man in a traditional toga stepped to the front of the platform to stand before the crowd, his purple sash and the brilliant white of his toga screaming *wealth and power*. Well, he was a senator. Julius wondered if that was his standard dress or if it was for the audience's sake.

Blasted out by the loudspeakers and hastily erected speakerphones set up the night before, the senator's voice echoed through the plaza as he too blabbered on endlessly about duty and moral fortitude. After the seventh mention of his (indubitably distant) relation to Emperor Julius Caesar, some nearby attendant must have given him the 'wrap it up' signal, because he got down to business with, "I now have the distinct honor—no, no, indeed—the *privilege* to introduce your new commanding officer, crusher of the Danube uprising and victor over the cowardly Persians at Tbilisi, Legate General Kruscus Minnicus!"

There was a loud roar of approval from the audience, recruits and citizens alike. *Are they cheering the end of the senator's speech, or for the general?* Julius wondered, squinting past red banners stamped with the gold Laurel Crown being waved between him and the tiny figure on the platform far above. Rows of medals on his crisp red and brown uniform glinted dully in the overcast light, overshadowed by the clean white strap that crossed his chest from right shoulder to left hip to hold his dress sword.

Minnicus adjusted his white gloves as he stepped up to the podium. "Friends, Romans, countrymen, my future soldiers and comrades-in-arms. I will keep my remarks brief, as we have training to begin and a war to prepare. I'm sure many of you are here with the idea of gaining glory and honor as a member of the XIII Germania. That is true! Under my leadership, we will add our names and banner to the halls of the Basilica Maximus in Rome.

"Look around! We are but small humans beside giants in the form of our mighty land, sea, and air creations. But it is we who give them strength and power, for without us, they are merely heaps of metal. You all know your country has need of you. A true Roman is selfless, and rises to defend his nation in a time of great need. I promise you today, that when you have grown old and have retired from the legion, you will be able to look back and say, 'We were true Romans.'"

As the crowd exploded in cheers and shouts, centurions and other officers moved through the crowd in the plaza, rounding up various groups of men to move them out of the city. Julius waved goodbye as he caught one last glimpse of his parents and little sister. In a small way, he already missed them. But it was time to move beyond this city. Now that he'd committed himself to the army, he almost felt driven by a desire to be doing something bigger with his life. He wouldn't be like the rest of the hapless, toiling, lower class, wasting his life working sunrise to sunset in a mechaniphant factory.

A centurion gestured at him, and Julius pushed his way over to the man. Several other men were already there.

"You, you, you, and all of you men there, put these on your shoulder," the centurion said, handing out double handfuls of tin Aquila pins with green slashes painted over the emblems.

Julius accepted the stack from the man next to him, passed the rest on to the man on his other side, then pinned his badge to his shoulder as the soldier continued his speech, his voice carrying through the crowd.

"I am Senior Centurion Vibius. Welcome to the green cohort. If you pass training, you will become members of the 13th Cohort, XIII Legion. We are the luckiest of the lucky, my boys. Keep up with me as we leave the city. You'll meet your commanding officer later. If you can't keep up, I'll just assume you dropped out and were too wimpy to become a real Roman."

Almost an hour passed before the recruits actually moved out. By then the entire city lined the Via Germanica to see off the future soldiers. It was both heartwarming and heartbreaking in a way. Never before had Julius experienced such an outpouring of enthusiasm from all levels of society. Certainly, as lovers and brothers and fathers left, there was an undertone of sadness and regret, but through it all ran a note of hope, the hope of a young man marching to war, plunder, and riches.

Streamers floated on the air and stirring, patriotic music played from every street corner, pub, restaurant, and public loudspeaker. Although the sights and smells kept tugging at Julius, he knew he would never have been able to work his way back onto the parade route to catch up with the rest of his training cohort if he left the column.

The Eastern Wall Gate loomed before them, festooned with all manner of defensive armaments, ropes, pulleys, chains, cranes, and open-frame elevators. Large flags bearing the gold Laurel Crown on a field of red hung down the wall on either side of the gate. Julius could see the tiny faces of lookouts high up on the wall, peeking between crenellations topping the battlements.

They marched into the dark tunnel through the curtain wall, the way illuminated by several sputtering gas lanterns hung temporarily on the tunnel walls and supplemented by the warm glow of crackling torches. They didn't provide much light, but Julius figured that there was only one direction to go. His eyes gradually adjusted as they shuffled along, spurred on by the voices of their officers. He looked up and saw murder holes and portcullis lines, darker areas in the dark ceiling, then stumbled and focused on placing his feet to avoid the metal train tracks that ran through the tunnel. *Why aren't we taking a train or steam hauler?* He wondered. *Is this part of the training? Or is it simply a way to wean out all the lazybones who can't even walk a few leagues?*

"I don't know about you, but I don't think I'd like coming back through this tunnel as an attacker," the man walking next to him said. In the dimly lit tunnel, he was a black outline with few identifying features to distinguish him from the multitude of other men moving through the tunnel.

"No way, not without a half-dozen walkers and maybe an assault caterpillar," Julius agreed.

The man clapped him on the back. "Ha! I'm still not sure I'd even want to try it with a full legion at my back!" His gruff, barking laugh echoed down the shaft, mingling with the voices of hundreds of other recruits. "I'm in yellow cohort," he added. "Name's Silenius. Used to be a carpenter by trade, but then got in trouble with some debt collectors. Joining the army is my way out. What training cohort did you get placed in?"

"Green."

"Oh. Well, good luck, then. You're the 13th of the 13th—it can't get any unluckier than that!" Again Silenius clapped him on the back. "I'm sure I'll see you around. After all, they make us fight each other to earn our place in the legion."

As the man moved off into the bright light at the end of the tunnel, for the first time, Julius wondered what exactly he had gotten himself into.

CHAPTER

3

C OLD RAIN SPLATTERED ON JULIUS'S face. It trickled down his cheeks, dripped off his sodden clothing, and slid down his arms to fall from his numb fingertips. Each quiet breath of air he drew released a puff of mist in front of him as he exhaled, a condition repeated a multitude of times around him. Julius could hear the teeth of Recruit Adueinus chattering next to him. He was surprised he could hear them over his own chattering teeth.

The legion recruits stood at attention on the massive drill ground, their feet covered in mud, their shoulders struggling to remain squared under the weight of heavy cloaks donned to ward off the unseasonably cool weather and the rain. Instead they seemed to absorb the cold along with the moisture as drill centurions marched the recruits around in the weather. Julius let his eyes stray wistfully in the direction of his barracks in the perfectly partitioned Roman military camp surrounding the drill ground.

Although the camp's layout followed one that had remained unchanged for the last three hundred years, Fort Tiberius was a more permanent fortification, so black-painted, prefabricated buildings had been erected in place of the canvas tents used on campaigns. The wall that surrounded it all was temporary, built from expandable wall segments carried by the men and wagon trains. The collapsible segments could be erected in half the time and were ten times as strong as a wooden palisade.

Julius realized his mind was wandering when Drill Centurion Haradan, one of the toughest, most grizzled, and intense instructors at Fort Tiberius appeared in front of him.

"RECRUIT HOW-LONG-SHOULD-IT-TAKE-FOR-A-SINGLE-COHORT-TO-BUILD-A-STANDARD-LEGION-CAMP?" Haradan shouted rapid-fire in Julius's face.

Julius's stomach squished up into his throat and he felt his knees shake. "CENTURION," he bellowed, "a single cohort should be able to build a standard camp in three hours, SIR!" He snapped his mouth shut, hoping the centurion would find no fault with his answer.

"Should? SHOULD? ARE YOU TELLING ME THAT SOME OF MY LEGIONARIES WILL NOT BE ABLE TO FINISH IN THREE HOURS? THAT YOU ARE TOO LAZY TO BUILD SOMETHING THAT COULD SAVE YOUR LIVES IN UNDER THREE HOURS? RECRUIT, IF I TELL YOU TO BUILD SOMETHING IN THREE HOURS, BY THE GODS, IT WILL BE DONE IN JUST ONE HOUR. THIS IS NOT SUMMER CAMP!"

The sheer volume of Haradan's response was overpowering. Beside Julius, Recruit Adueinus released a small whimper that drew Haradan's attention, and Julius slowly released his pent breath. As Haradan started bellowing at Adueinus, Julius wondered if this part of training was meant to teach recruits to recognize and hear orders over the din of battle. In this case, though, the "battle" was fifteen or so drill instructors yelling, questioning, verbally abusing, and insulting the 13th Recruit Cohort, each one fighting to be louder than the others. And the "battle" was viciously one-sided.

With an inner smile, Julius noted that even Tribune Appius, 13th Cohort's commanding officer, was receiving a similar heckling on the status of his cohort. Constantine seemed to be holding up pretty well. He even wore the blank-eyed stare that the recruits had quickly learned to adopt, his eyes straight ahead, apparently completely ignoring the red-faced drillmaster shouting in his ear. He was facing the legion, Senior Centurion Vibius at his side. Julius had originally been unaware that new cohorts and their leaders were required to train together, to better foster a sense of camaraderie and trust. Of course, it also led to a sharing of skills, knowledge, and, in this case, blame. Julius allowed the inner smile to creep over his face.

In the blink of an eye, Drill Centurion Haradan was back in front of him. "DO YOU THINK STANDING OUT HERE IS FUNNY, HONEY BUN? WHY ARE YOU SMILING? GET DOWN IN THE MUD AND GIVE ME FIFTY."

Julius sighed inwardly as he knelt in the mud and dropped forward onto his hands for push-ups. He couldn't remember the last time he had taken a hot bath, or slept, or even eaten, for that matter. He lowered his body into the mud, and then straightened his arms. His body ached from the weight of the segmented body armor he'd been wearing day in and day out.

"YOU BRAINLESS WIMP! I DIDN'T HEAR ANY COUNTING. START OVER!"

Julius groaned inwardly and started bellowing off a count.

~ * * * ~

"Never, in all my years as a drill centurion, have I *ever* had such an incompetent, worthless, idiotic cohort to deal with. I doubt you could find your bootlaces if you had a manual and a guide! I trust you aren't hoping that being related to our most glorious emperor is going to get you out of this one." The instructor's voice was raw, and it seemed to compound the misery of the day.

Constantine was glad that the rain continued to fall. That way, no one could see the single tear sneaking down his cheek. He was embarrassed by the whole operation. Deep down, he knew he had failed in his responsibility. Just where had today's operation gone so completely and horribly wrong?

The ten squads of 13th Cohort, XIII Germania Legion, had marshaled and left their quarters around six on a bright, cool morning and waited in column formation for the day's exercise, this one relatively simple: march to a location, build a temporary fort, take down the fort, then march back to their quarters. The raw light of a new day shone over them, though the gray clouds promised rain later.

The men were carrying all the necessary gear. The Roman army had replaced the traditional wooden crossframe with an expandable haversack, each haversack containing three days worth of rations, an axe, a wrench, several extra nuts and bolts, and that man's fort component. In total, the pack weighed about fifty pounds. Added to this weight were mock double-weight wooden plumbata (the real ones had not yet been distributed), the full complement of steel and ceramic armor plating for his shoulders and chest, his helmet, a full-size *scuta* shield, and his utility belt. Now the average recruit was carrying upwards of ninety pounds worth of material.

Accompanied by a single drill instructor, the 13th marched in a line three abreast, with Tribune Appius in the front rank. He could already feel the impact the program of constant conditioning was having on his body. His arms had gained muscle mass, and his frame had slimmed down. Long marches had improved his endurance and fortitude. Today's march was no exception. He appreciated that his fitness level meant he no longer focused on his body's struggles and complaints; it freed him to turn his thoughts and observations outward.

Those may have industrialized agriculture and increased food production across the empire, but they're awkward-looking contraptions, Constantine thought as they marched past massive wheat-harvesting machines working the field next to the road. He watched a massive scythe on the nearest machine sweep left to right through the stalks before it, then followed the cut wheat with his eyes as it was carried up a conveyor belt that rotated it up almost like a waterwheel into a container in the back part of the thresher machine. The farmer sitting in the driver's seat waved down at them, and he lifted a hand, then jumped with several other soldiers when a loud hiss of steam erupted from the machine. He smiled at the brief fit of laughter around him.

A few miles into the march, Constantine listened to the low conversation of the men directly behind him, arguing the merits of the mechaniphant versus the combat tortoise. Both machines were cornerstones of Imperial Rome's military successes. That, plus its air squadrons of dirigibles and powered gliders, had allowed Rome to dominate Europe, the Mediterranean, the Balkans, North Africa, and the Near East for hundreds of years. Several of his legionnaires seemed to have come from the great factories of Brittenburg that churned out these metal behemoths, or had assembled the heavy ballistae and steam catapults that armed them. The discussion was lively, and it helped Constantine, like the men behind him, to pass the time and make the miles unnoticed.

"Only the gods would dare try to attack something like that on foot," rumbled fifth squad's leader, Sergeant Decimus. "I'd rather sit a mile away and hit it with a repeating ballista armed with explosive bolts. That'd take it down, no problem."

"The mechaniphant would just crush the attackers flat," someone stated with an air of finality, and the resulting discussion involved whether or not such an event could occur.

The 13th Cohort rounded a bend in the road, and Constantine heard the soft, soothing burble of water over rocks. He pulled off his helmet with one hand and wiped his brow with the other, smudging the dirt the dusty air had left on his forehead. With the sweat out of his eyes, he could better see the condition of the stone bridge crossing the small stream just ahead of him. It was about five feet high, obviously one of the original Roman military construction projects in this part of the countryside, though it had aged well, with only a few stones loose or damaged. He looked around. He could see a fair distance in the flat countryside, spying some small windmills and smokestacks far off. The *chuff-chuff-chuff* of a steamtractor came from somewhere off to the east.

"What are you thinking, sir?" Centurion Vibius asked. He checked his chronometer. "We're supposed to be at the junction by one o'clock."

Constantine winced inwardly. He hated it when the man acted like his nursemaid. The man's propensity to be right—about everything—annoyed him. *Just remember,* he wanted to say, *I am the one in command.* "We'll take a ten minute break. Ninth squad will be on lookout, rotated out with 10th squad," he told Vibius. *So there; I'm the one in charge!*

"Yes, sir," Vibius responded, his face a blank. He moved off make the arrangements.

Drill Instructor Vespasinus flipped open his brass-covered observation notebook and Constantine watched the dark-skinned Cretan scribble in it as he circled their position, noting the placements of the guards and the time. Constantine swallowed. The man had spent twenty years as a legionnaire, and so was considered an excellent judge of a man's worth. His report would weigh heavily on the future prospects of Tribune Constantine Tiberius Appius.

Now sweaty from the half-day march, many of the men sank to the ground, some pulling off their *nova caligae* to massage their feet. Though standard issue was no longer the sandal-like shoe design of yore, the shin-high leather boots reinforced with flexible strips of metal and an iron toe were still just that—new shoes to be broken in. Others wobbled over to the river to fill their helmets with water and pour it over their heads.

A few began splashing water playfully at each other, water droplets glistening in the bright sunlight. Jostling escalated to shoving between a pair of hot-heads, and more and more recruits got dragged into the burgeoning brawl. Eventually, Recruit Dapelicus swung a beautiful left hook that rocked Recruit Horatio most of the way out of the water and onto the pebble-strewn shore. The situation deteriorated from there.

Constantine was quietly conferring with Vespasinus over the finer points of guard posts and regulations when a legionnaire scrambled up the slight rise, hastily saluted, and made his report on the situation.

"Very well. Go get 9th and 10th squads. Tell them to be here on the double. Then find the drill instructor."

"Yes, sir!" The recruit took off at full speed, no small feat for a man not yet accustomed to wearing the full legionary kit.

Constantine and Vespasinus turned and booted it toward the small stream, where Constantine waded into the thick of the fight, trying to separate the combatants. His yells did nothing to quash the melee. A fist swung out of nowhere and hit him full in the gut.

It felt like all the air had gone out of his body. His vision swam and he tasted the sharp, acidic tang of bile in his mouth. His knees wanted to give out. Instead, his combat senses kicked in, honed from many a fight with both his older brother and drill instructors back at the palace.

Constantine grabbed the hand of the man who had swung at him and yanked him back, left hand pulling hard on the legionary's wrist. His right hand pulled out his flare launcher, a newer piece of equipment loaded with a one-time shot of bright red firework. He used the launcher as a club, bringing it down on the man's head. Blood spurted as the man's nose shattered. The man's hands went to his face and he sank to the ground beside the stream, water lapping around his ankles.

Constantine heard his name called as he stood looking down at the recruit and turned, wiping some of the man's blood off his cheek. Ducking out of the way of a flying helmet, he saw Centurion Vibius using his sword, still in the scabbard, to bludgeon his way through to Constantine. Both turned when they heard a shout from the top of the nearby hill.

Ninth and 10th squads were assembled at the top of the rise, their weapons at the ready; at the order to charge from the instructor beside them, their armored lines now advanced on the melee in the stream.

Constantine looked around him. *All these idiots—how can I become a hero if I can't get these blithering numbskulls to finish a gods-damned training mission!* Fed up, he aimed the launcher at the sky and pulled the trigger.

A bright red streak shot upward. The flare then exploded, leaving a blast of red as an afterimage on the inside of Constantine's eyelids. He blinked in time to see the puff of red smoke that floated gracefully on the light wind.

The brawling stopped as combatants froze, then hastily stepped away from each other with guilty looks. Constantine glared at them. "What, in Pluto's name, do you think you are doing?" he shouted. "Form up—*immediately*! Centurion Vibius, sound roll call. Any man not able to stand at attention will be assigned to punishment detail."

The roll call left eight men down on the ground, some unconscious, others actually injured. One of those was the man Constantine had clubbed with his flare gun.

Constantine raked his eyes over the shambles of his cohort, many dripping wet and sporting fresh bruises, their clothing torn. "I have only one simple question. Who started this mess?" A flurry of blame, finger pointing, and general whining ensued. Constantine sighed. *Did I sign up to play babysitter to a bunch of school children?*

"If you insist on tattling, I will have to put you all in a time-out," Vibius said. The off-hand statement hit the men like a freight train. The assembled recruits stared at the older centurion, hatred fighting with fear in their eyes.

The leader of 9th squad, a large, rotund man with a red handlebar mustache, laughed heartily at the centurion's comment. His laugh carried over the field. "Good one, sir! Those ninnies need a sit-down 'fore they can play at real soldiers!"

Constantine ignored the comments. He had lost their attention, and was not sure what to do to regain it. Instructor Vespasinus was furiously writing notes in his notebook. Distressed, Constantine fumbled for something to say. *Ancestors, give me an inspirational, but firm, speech!*

Fortunately (or, as it seemed later, unfortunately), his thoughts were interrupted by a large, oblong shadow moving across the ground. He, along with his entire unit, looked up to see a small airship blocking the weak sun as it clawed its way through the clouds. A woman stood out front on a catwalk, with a curious object held up to her face.

Centurion Vibius immediately moved in front of the tribune, perhaps sensing that the ship was up to no good. Constantine motioned at his two equipped squads, trying to get them to stand down. Finally they understood his gestures, and the 9th and 10th squads tried hastily to look as unassuming as possible.

The airship circled the cohort and descended. When Constantine could see the red letters painted on over three-fourths of the airship's side, he nearly cried out in frustration. *Ravenna Chronicle. Damn.*

"Who is that?" one of the men assembled on the banks of the stream asked.

"The most ignorant, yellow-tongued, filthy, lowly men in the world," Centurion Vibius responded. Vespasinus paused in his writing and looked up, wearing a confused expression.

"Nortlanders?" someone asked.

"No" Constantine responded, almost in a whisper, "*reporters.*"

Later that afternoon, the 13th Cohort, XIII Germania Legion, staggered into Fort Tiberius, carrying their eight injured men back from their exercise on improvised stretchers they had lashed together. They had been unable to complete the training mission due to their injuries, lost time, and the arrival of the *Ravenna Chronicle* airship, *Headline.* The ship had buzzed around them for about an hour, the people on board obviously taking pictures and enjoying the discomfort of the men on the ground.

Instructor Vespasinus informed the tribune that he was to make a full report on the situation. Which was how the company now found itself standing in the cold rain facing the wrath of a dozen or so instructors. Although the iron discipline that had built the Roman army into a formidable force still existed, the punishment methods had been modified. The men had to stand at attention for the remainder of the day, officers included.

Several hours later, the exhausted members of the 13th Cohort stumbled into their barracks hall to collapse upon their beds, only a few managing to shed their wet armor and clothes before falling down.

Constantine entered the barracks after them. "Men, I have something to tell you," he said in a voice that carried to the end of the hall. "I know it's late, but this is critical information that is important for you know tonight.

"I understand how you are feeling right now. You are angry and upset, but most of all, you are tired. The biggest deal today was not the fight, nor was it that our instructor watched us act like bulls fighting it out over a cow. Rather, it was that the newspaper got photographs of us in a poor situation. Not only does it reflect badly upon the army, but it also reflects poorly upon my family."

He took a breath. This was his most tightly held secret, and he wasn't completely sure he had made the right decision in trusting these men.

The hall was silent, his men staring at him, undisguised discontent on their faces. "Why should we care how that reflects upon your family, sir?" one of them asked, his tone angry and resentful. "If they are rich enough to purchase your position, they're rich enough to get through a bad broadsheet story. Sorry, sir, but your family will just have to deal with it, like the rest of us commoners."

Murmurs swept through the unit. "Let the man speak. Then you judge," Centurion Vibius spoke up from the corner; Constantine hadn't noticed him enter.

Constantine nodded his thanks. He took a deep breath. "You may have noticed that my name is similar to some very famous Romans"

"That's not uncommon, sir; all of my names were taken from famous Romans, as well. It's a bit annoying, honestly," the same man interjected.

Constantine inclined his head toward the recruit. "Recruit Julius Caesar, correct? I remember you from earlier today. And yes, that may be true, but in my case, I'm actually a living descendent of those famous Romans. My full name and title is Constantine Tiberius Appius, *Secundus Imperio,* or second in line for the Laurel Crown and the throne of the Roman Empire, and all dependent vassals, tributaries, and colonies. As you can see, I'm not walking around with bodyguards, nor do I have a train of servants a mile long. If you're looking for that, I think my older brother is back in Rome." He flashed a quick smile as he looked around the room, getting lukewarm chuckles in return.

"I'm here to ask your help—your help in continuing a battle long waged between the forces of order and the forces opposed. It began with my ancestor, the first emperor, Julius Caesar himself, as he ravaged the Gauls and crushed their resistance in battle after battle. Order prevailed over chaos. This is our heritage. Cornelia, Caesar's wife, bore him two sons, long after our priests said she was infertile. Once again, order prevailed, and created a dynasty. Those sons established the seeds that began our efforts to harness nature to our engine of empire. We discovered anthracite coal and its powers, learned the secrets of the Persians, the Egyptians, the Indians, and the Chinese. We crafted mechanical monstrosities and graceful airships. Our mechaniphants decimated the United German tribes in the Teutonburg under Emperor Titus Octavian, and once again, the order of Rome was triumphant." He paused for a moment, looking at his men.

They were tired, but they *seemed* to understand the importance of this situation. Their officer was asking them to help continue the strength that was Rome through their efforts, while following a scion of the dynasty that had founded the empire they had sworn to serve.

"That victory over the Germans is only one instance of the industrial might of Rome, and its legions, succeeding where others had failed. We forced those Nortland barbarians across the Vistula, planted multiple *colonia* in the new world, and have established the most technologically superior air and sea fleet ever seen." His voice echoed through the barracks, the men being drawn into his speech, his words, his utmost *belief* in the ideas he was talking about. Constantine was crafting a living, breathing empire that was as much theirs as it was his creation.

"But should we stand complacent? Rest on our laurels? We cannot!" Constantine roared. "Nortland pecks at us like that raven god they worship—a raid here, a raid there. They would love to get their hands on some of our fair cities. Will you allow that?"

"No!" the men cheered and catcalled in response.

"Will you allow those chaotic forces to wrest from us these fertile fields and forests we've worked to make our own? And what of our eastern borders? The Mongolian Crimearate has long burned and pillaged their way toward us. The Chinese could not stop them. The Indians, the Persians—they all *failed!* But not us, not we Romans! My great-uncle, General Augustus Belisarius, held the Mongols off for weeks, using the holy river Jordan as his battle line. Their horse archers were no match for our airships. Greek fire cares little for sand or water, and even less for the antics of those nomadic barbarians."

He dropped his voice, drawing in every man in the room. "But they have learned from us, learned some of our technology, some of our skills. Will we give them an opening? A chance to rob and pillage and burn and destroy? We've stopped them once, but I doubt that will be the last we see of them."

He turned back toward the door. "Will you give them the chance? The chance to tear down all that we've built? Take millennia of blood, sweat, and tears and simply let it go? Or will you help me fight for it, help us to keep alive the belief, the idea, the power that is Rome?" His rhetorical question had only one answer, and his men all knew it. To give up would be tantamount to surrender.

Legions don't surrender.

"I only ask that you try your hardest, give it your all, demonstrate your loyalty and strength in every way. When those reporters were here today, that blew part of my cover. They will try to get spies in here to try and embarrass the royal family. I'm sure by now they are already cranking out insane leaflets about the horrors and abuses I'm subjecting you to here during training—or better yet, my lack of skill as an officer. But to be honest, I couldn't care less about my family name. I would feel ashamed if my actions dishonored this legion."

Constantine stopped in the doorway, and looked out onto the rain-drenched training fields. "It's time to decide. What will you choose—order and prosperity, or chaos and destruction?"

One of his recruits—Julius, Constantine recalled—looked around. "Sir, I don't speak for all of us" he stated, "but I know what I think. I'm loyal to the Empire and to you, sir." He ended abruptly, but that was all that needed to be said.

For a moment, blue eyes met brown. An unspoken message of support passed between the two men.

"Thank you," Constantine said. "Now get some sleep, men; we've got weapons drills in the morning." His back straight, Constantine turned and marched out of the room. Vibius saluted him as he exited, then turned smartly on his heels and marched out as well. In his heart, Constantine knew he had made the right, and the only, decision possible. Outside, the moonbeams finally pushed through the retreating storm clouds, bringing light to the darkness.

~ * * * ~

Back inside the barracks, quiet conversations sprang up almost immediately after the tribune's departure.

"Anyone actually believe that swine slop?" Recruit Traxion sneered to the bunkmates gathered conspiratorially around him.

"Seems like the others bought it," another recruit observed, looking around the barracks.

Green eyes flashing anger, Traxion swatted him across the head, rocking him back onto the squeaky bunk. "They're just mindless drones, blinded by their subservience to the Empire," he said, his sarcastic voice mildly singsong, as if mouthing political dogma. Color flushed his pale cheeks, making him appear almost embarrassed at the vehemence of his own statement.

His comrades looked at each other uncertainly, and remained silent. "Don't worry, I'll have a few friends take care of this problem," Traxion continued smugly. Taking the cue, his men began to chuckle, and a slow smile stretched his lips. "Oh yes, I think they'll be overjoyed to hear of our tribune's parentage."

CHAPTER

4

I T WAS OFTEN SAID THAT even the fog feared to tread in the depths of Sludge Bottom. Only the brave, the foolhardy, the desperate, or the conniving dared to venture into that economically stagnant and most run-down sector of Brittenburg, where seedy gambling halls, dank, smoke-filled bars, and automaton-fighting pits in abandoned warehouses were the chief attractions. The operators of these businesses, always tight-fisted and tight-lipped, had tightened their vigilance as well, with the auxilia more active recently. Anyone who seemed a bit out of place or a tad too eager to learn more about their companions at the gambling table was "taken care of," right along with anyone who happened to develop an exceptionally strong winning streak at the dice tables or during a rigged card game.

Here, Domino Grex ran the notorious Atrium, five stories of every kind of disreputable entertainment imaginable. The building stank of desperation and ill-gotten gains. The fact that it was neither as well-lit nor as well-ventilated as its name implied appealed to the con artists, runaway peasants, prostitutes, loan sharks, and the city's assorted riff-raff who frequented the establishment. And no one crossed Grex. The survival rate for those who did was zero. Even the auxilia dared not raid the place. Domino Grex had so many illicit connections that his complex was untouchable; any officer who tried to impose the law soon found himself transferred to the city's Sanitary Division.

Though the private rooms on the fifth floor could provide for any vice or perversion, they seemed to exude the evil, hatred, anger, and violence they'd witnessed over the years. No member of Grex's staff was assigned up there for any length of time. Too many seemed to disappear, go mad, or simply see things that … shouldn't … be there.

One of the largest of these rooms had been booked for the evening. Two muscular street toughs stood on either side of a dented copper door, the verdigris of age belying its well-oiled mechanisms. The men leaned on heavy clubs, and short swords and daggers were sheathed at their belts. The toughs stepped together in front of the door as three cloaked figures approached, blocking their passage.

The cloaked figures each withdrew necklaces from within their cowls to display small medallions with intricately geared moving components. Newly alert eyes lighting up their dull expressions, the thugs nodded to one another and moved aside to let the strangers pass. The leader inserted his medallion into an opening in the wall as if it were a key; after an audible hum, the door hissed open, sliding slowly into the wall. The figures passed between the two toughs, who ignored them—their job was to guard the door; what happened inside was not their business.

With another hiss, the door squealed shut behind the last cloaked figure to enter, and the gaslights blazed in their wall sconces, casting a yellowish haze throughout the room. Two of the figures moved to the last remaining high-backed chairs surrounding a massive brass table, designed in the shape of a gear, in the center of the room. The third figure stood between and slightly behind the two chairs, keeping his face in shadow. Anticipation weighted the air, seeming to make movement a challenge.

One of the cloaked figures already at the table pulled a dagger from within the depths of his cloak and rapped its pommel three times on the tabletop, making the ruby liquid jump in the wine pitcher surrounded by glasses in the center of the table. "Let this meeting come to order. *Deus Ex Mortalitas!* From the gods comes death," he intoned. "We are the hand of that death—the death of the abomination that is the Roman Empire. So has it been decreed by our gods. Let us hear the words of our leader, Brimmas Amalia." He sheathed his dagger as all heads turned toward the newcomers.

The voice that emerged from the folds of that black cloak was feminine, cold, and precise. "Let us reveal ourselves, for all of us here are friends in a cause that is just and right and worthy of each other's trust." She lifted pale hands to push back her hood, revealing a narrow face with thin lips set in a perpetual expression of disapproval, and piercing blue eyes. Only crow's-feet at the corners of her eyes and lines framing her mouth suggested her age. Her colorless face appeared to float within the shadowy blackness of her curly hair.

The others revealed themselves as well—several dignified-looking older men, a woman with several chins, an average-looking man with ink-stained hands, and a gentleman with a brass monocle clenched over his eye. Several young men, barely out of their teens, completed the assembled group. Amalia's seated companion lowered his hood as well, and the yellow gaslight gleamed on his clean-shaven head. Between the bald pate and a full, coarse brown beard, level brown eyes drank in every detail and aspect of the room.

"The Romans are corrupting this land," Amalia hissed. "They abuse good citizens. They tax us until we cannot support our own families. These are facts; they are not new to us. Nor are they new to any citizen of the Roman Empire. Yet the people dare not fight back against the iron heel of the Empire and its monolithic bureaucracy. They have forgotten how to resist, how to strike back at the corruptors and defilers of our lands and our heritage." She paused and swept the gathering with her eyes. "The rabble has forgotten, but we have not. We shall strike, and we shall be victorious. This city will make the perfect example of our new power. For when we have torn her from the grasp of the Romans, no one will doubt our resolve, and the masses will flock to us in droves, eager to turn against their corrupt leaders and elitist masters."

The others at the table nodded as she spoke.

"Independently, we control several different, but unorganized, branches of this city that could benefit from the elimination of Imperial controls. Together, working simultaneously toward the same goals, we are unstoppable. The industrialists," she nodded toward the three men in expensive-looking tunics and cloaks. "have provided us with the walkers and weapons we need to take on the auxilia and the governor's lackeys face to face."

"With adequate compensation and ... destruction of our rivals' workshops during the uprising," one industrialist responded, languorously waving his hand.

Amalia nodded, then inclined her head toward the portly woman. "Domina Aurelia has provided us with ample ... insight into the actions and anticipated procedures of the auxilia and other security forces."

The woman's double chins jiggled as she bobbed her head up and down. "Boys can never keep their mouths shut when they are occupied elsewhere." She giggled.

"We even have friends in Rome who are ready to act on our behalf." Amalia pointed at the monocled man without identifying him. He was a stranger to the others. "Do you have any updates?"

"I believe we can successfully eliminate both the emperor and the *primus imperio,* his heir apparent. We can also destroy their long-range communications equipment, as well as cut the telegraph lines."

"What about the other heir? I would think security around him would be less challenging to penetrate." The industrialist rubbed a bejeweled hand over his balding head. "Why not just eliminate every male family member while we're at it?"

"Because we aren't sure where he is," the monocled man replied, his voice condescending. "We know he came through Brittenburg, and we know that he is working with the XIII

Germania Legion up at Fort Tiberius. We do not have sufficient contacts in place there, and communication in and out is strictly regulated. I've been waiting for a source to report in for a while. He has not been on liberty, as my men would have reported it."

"I'm fairly certain that the only reason you know he's there for sure is because that newspaper managed to photograph him," an industrialist said with a sneer. "Not very good espionage, if you ask me."

The monocled man stood, the optical glass dropping the length of its golden chain as his eyes widened. His fists pounded the table and he glared, red-faced, at the man.

Before he could unleash a barrage of insults at the factory owner, Amalia interrupted. "Gentlemen, please stop your incessant arguing. It does none of us any good." She turned her hawk-like gaze on the monocled man. "Now Chalbys, you've done an excellent job. There will be plenty of opportunities to get at the second son. And frankly, if we play our cards right here and in Rome, we will be able to eliminate his ability to take charge. The squabbling among the Senate and the plebeians will cause chaos in the streets. It might even overwhelm the Praetorian Guard and the Urban Cohort. At the very least, the High Command will be forced into a tricky situation: hold out for the second son, hoping he can take charge in time to prevent far-flung parts of the Empire from collapsing, or mount a coup. Either way, Rome will truly be at the mercy of the mob."

Her attempt to soothe the angry Chalbys worked; the man sat back down. She turned to the young men fidgeting at the end of the table. "We are very close to dealing the first of many blows for the people. We have yet to hear from our youngest team members. How goes recruitment?"

The response came in mostly slang Latin, barely understandable to some of those higher up the social ladder. "We gotsa 'bout 'undred 'ore Sludgeheads. Deyre meane and nastay, but we be ready for day victory of da workers. Mayb' we hunt dem auxilia, 'stead of dey huntin' us."

When several of those around the table snorted at his speech, the gang chieftain scowled and pulled out a gleaming chain knife. The miniature battery sparked to life and the steel teeth began to whir around. "Whose be laufen at meh?" he growled. His companions also began to reach for hidden weapons.

"*Stop. Now,*" Amalia commanded. Her voice froze those at the table. "Sit, and let us discuss ways to harm the Romans, instead of each other."

"It is past time for Operation Teutonburg to move beyond the planning stage. I want all operations in motion. I want gang recruitment doubled within two weeks. Everyone will await word of the assassination. Whether it has happened or not, we move on this date." She pointed to a date circled in red on a small calendar she had removed from her belt pouch. She passed it around the table. "Keep this date in your memory. On this date you will receive a message reminding you of your commitments and requirements. If you shirk or if you renege, you will be removed. However, if you stand with us, as you have promised, you will receive a place in the new order. You will be rewarded beyond your wildest dreams." Her voice edged higher. The committee members glanced at one another.

"And the Imperials?" an industrialist asked, almost in a whisper.

"They will be fractured. A Rome turned upon itself is unable to rule. With no central government and no live heir, the governors will at first be unsure what to do. Some may be convinced to come to our side. Others can be eliminated. Others may discover they like ruling as a king or emperor, rather than paying tribute to Rome. Rome will falter, and the weak provinces will wither on the vine, denied the ability to suckle on the largesse of Rome." Amalia's words rang from the stone walls that wept condensation around them.

"But how can we face the legions?" the ink-stained man asked. He was a scribe working in the governor's office, well placed to hear and redirect anything of note. "We don't have their training, their equipment, or, to be perfectly honest, their experience."

Murmurs rose around the table. The gang chieftains leapt up, protesting the implication that they were weak and untrained. One brandished his chain knife. Noting the spirals of dragons chasing each other heavily tattooed on his scarred arm, Amalia recognized the intricate, gem-flecked mark of the Extraxi street gang, the most powerful, debauched, and ruthless of the gangs in the city. Glaring a warning at them, she lifted her hand off the table, crooking one finger. "Corbus, please remove our friends' weaponry from this meeting; they have no need of it."

The man in the shadows behind her moved. In barely the blink of an eye, he appeared behind the three gangers. A clatter of weaponry and several shouts and thumps later, two of the three gang chieftains lay in a heap on the floor, moaning and cursing at the hooded man. The last man sat holding his bleeding nose. Their weapons were nowhere in sight.

"As you can see, my son is a fine warrior," Amalia said. "He will help lead us. As the descendent of the great Germanic freedom fighter Arminius, he has the blood of heroes and warriors in his veins. He will not let us down. Nor, I think, will our Nortland allies. I have arranged for assistance from them on the date we have set. Thus, everything must be prepared appropriately." She stared around at her fellow conspirators. "What say you?"

They slid back their chairs and rose to bow deeply toward the seated Amalia. She released a mental sigh. She had feared that she would have to coerce them into accepting her plan, but now she could save those tactics for later, when the truly squeamish balked at the idea of suborning, distracting, or murdering Imperial officials and soldiers. *That will be the time for force,* she thought. *To bind them to us, by making us the only alternative to death or destruction. Only then will we have their full loyalty.*

As the other seditionists filed out of the Atrium's private chamber, a few cast covert glances back at Amalia and

Corbus, but she revealed nothing in her body language or facial expression that would give anything away, and Corbus waited stone-faced beside her.

When the last of them had left the room, Corbus turned to Amalia. She already had her hand raised, anticipating his question. "For the last time, child, they will follow us. I have no doubt in your ability to lead our men to victory. But you must continue to train them, every moment you have available. I have no expectation that you improve our fellow rebels to legionary status; your days as an auxilia constable are done. All I expect is that they can take on the city guard in a straight-up fight. You provide the tip of the assault, the ganger boys will provide the body."

Corbus nodded, then said in a deep voice that did not match his youthful appearance, "It is my duty, Mother. I understand our history. It's past time we took our revenge. We will make the streets slippery with blood and hang those corrupt dogs by their togas, as our ancestors would have demanded," he snarled.

"That's my boy, my Germanic champion," Amalia crooned. His eyes closed and he shivered. "Now, let's leave, and continue our preparations in a more suitable environment."

Again swathing themselves in their cloaks, they exited the room, slipped out of the Atrium, and faded into the anonymity of the Brittenburg night.

CHAPTER

5

G ATHER 'ROUND, GATHER 'ROUND, YOU men." Drill
Instructor Vespasinus held a length of steel and iron
up in front of him. "Anyone know what this is?" He
looked expectantly at the legionaries assembled around him.

"A plumbata," one of them answered, and several others
nodded.

"Yes. And what is that?" the instructor prodded.

Julius spoke up. "It's a short javelin that can explode on
contact. Or it can penetrate an enemy shield to slow their
attack."

"Good, good! Excellent answer, Recruit Caesar . That's
exactly what I was looking for. Each man in a legion is armed
with two of these weapons. But—" he looked around at the
green legionnaires "—the smart soldier always carries a few
more. There are two variations of plumbatae: the first tipped
with an explosive canister, the second topped with the
standard soft iron shank."

He moved over to the shooting range, where several straw
dummies awaited destruction. Grasping a plumbata in one
calloused hand, he said, "This shaft has a single-use
explosive component attached at the top. Our artificers and
engineers designed it so that it will explode upon direct,

forceful contact with a hard surface, most likely an enemy's armor, or his shield. Upon impact, the blast is funneled toward the enemy. It's strong enough to in all likelihood kill anyone within an eight-foot area, with a fragmentation radius twice that. It's reliable 95% of the time and, when used in combination with others, can sweep even an armored front line clear in a single volley."

Hefting the plumbata, he took a few quick steps and hurled it downrange. It struck one of the straw dummies in the torso. *Bang!* The dummy exploded into thousands of pieces. Bits of straw and canvas floated about in the air as pieces of jagged metal tinkled to the ground. The gathered legionaries cheered.

Vespasinus gave a half-bow and quipped, "Thank you, thank you, encore performance at seven for those interested. Now men, pick up a plumbata shaft. Each shaft has a screw attachment at the top." He gestured to several crates full of plumbatae that other instructors had opened with crowbars.

Julius walked over to the nearest crate and helped pass out several of the weapon shafts. Finally, he took one for himself and walked over to the rough line that the men had formed along the near end of the range.

"What I am showing you now are the two varieties of spearheads that can be placed on the plumbata," the instructor said, holding up a foot-long, finger-thick iron shank emerging from a cylindrical tub. He demonstrated screwing the shank onto the pole, then he unscrewed it. "That is the simple plumbata shaft. It will bend upon hitting an enemy shield, making the shield unwieldy and throwing the bearer off balance. Smart warriors will drop their shields. Dumb ones will carry the awkward weight along. Either way, you will have an advantage over them." He displayed a wolfish grin, and then tossed the plain plumbata shank to another instructor, who deftly snagged it out of midair.

Vespasinus began screwing a heavier diamond-shaped explosive tip onto the plumbata, saying, "Each component will attach to the shaft by way of the screw. This is a black gunpowder fragmentation warhead."

Other helpers walked along the line, passing out similar spearheads; Julius listened as he carefully screwed on the dangerous warhead he was given.

"The shafts are designed to withstand the pressure of the explosion. Realistically, they tend to take some damage, but about half of them can be reused. Remember, the trigger requires a straight hit; glancing ones won't do the trick." Turning, Drill Instructor Vespasinus stepped to one side and bellowed, "On my order! Ready plumbatae."

Julius and the others balanced their plumbatae on open palms next to their ears. Instructors scurried down the line, helping to adjust the position of each plumbata. Several men nearly dropped them, snatching them up at the last second. The instructor waited until they were all prepared before belting out his next words.

"A volley is far more devastating than a single hit, remember that! Now—ready, *THROW!*"

The missiles arced raggedly from their line, followed seconds later by a rolling series of explosions. Julius instinctively threw his hand up before his face as dust, dirt, and straw flew everywhere. When the explosions stopped, the instructor pulled a lever on the wall. A mechanical alarm sounded. Several large fans slowly blew the smoke and floating debris away so that the soldiers could see the results.

Julius gaped with the others. Wisps of smoke still rose gently from the craters where the straw dummies once stood. Vespasinus motioned, and the recruits followed him forward over the fragmented ground. Squatting, he scooped up a small piece of jagged metal, tossing it from hand to hand to cool it down. "This is what happens when the warhead on the plumbata explodes. The black powder is triggered by the impact. The outer casing shatters, sending hot pieces of iron into bodies and armor and shields. A single well-placed plumbata can even take down an airship. A volley of plumbatae will stagger an advancing enemy, wound their men, disorganize them, hurt their morale, and deal them a psychological blow." He delivered the speech in the cold, hard manner of a man who has seen it happen before.

He pointed to one of his students. "You, Recruit Gven ... Gwyen—What in Jupiter's beard is your name?" he finally snapped.

"Sir, it's pronounced Ven-durn; it's from my great-uncle."

Vespasinus tossed the piece of iron to Recruit Gwendyrn. "Sorry 'bout the horrible name. Now, if you please, imagine that going through your shin, Gwendyrn. At this instant, you're wounded, thrashing about, possibly even injuring other men with your movements. You're bleeding out and your comrades are worried about you, so they want to take you back to the medico." He looked around at the others, pointing to Gwendyrn. "How many men do you think it will take to get him back to a first aid station?"

Julius shrugged with the others, his leather tunic shifting on his shoulders.

"Get on the ground and let's see how people react to the situation," he told Gwendyrn. "Thrash around so it looks like you're injured."

Gwendyrn lay down and began feebly moving his legs. "Ouch, ouch!" he said with limited enthusiasm.

Instructor Vespasinus walked over to him. As the remaining recruits stood watching uncertainly, his leg swung back, then he kicked Gwendyrn right in the knee with his iron-toed nova caligae. Julius grimaced; that would leave a brutal bruise. Gwendyrn screamed and grabbed his knee, now writhing around in pain. Vespasinus stepped to one side and looked around. "What are you waiting for? Get him behind the line!"

Julius and several other recruits quickly reached down to lift the struggling man. An explosion suddenly erupted to their right.

"What was that?" Julius shouted, ducking over Gwendyrn's moaning, still writhing form. The other recruits had either crouched or dropped flat to the ground, below the trajectory of any shrapnel. The injured man was completely forgotten. Julius looked wildly at the instructor. "Was that an accident?"

"This is not some pansy walk in the forum, recruit!" Vespasinus yelled from the safety of the wall. "Get your armor-clad bodies in gear! Move, *move*, MOVE!"

Julius grabbed Gwendyrn's arm. Several other recruits grabbed the downed man and lifted him, then began dragging him toward the low wooden wall that separated the free fire part of the range from the safe part of the range. A plumbata went sailing over their heads, followed by another explosion. This time, Julius heard the whine of shrapnel behind him. "Go faster!" he cried out.

The men began to move together, more efficiently this time. The wall was twenty feet away. Then just fifteen feet. Then ten feet. Then they were moving Gwendyrn over the wall. The men gave a ragged cheer as he was lifted over.

"By Jupiter's beard, why'd you have to go and kick me, sir?" Gwendyrn groaned as he was helped to his feet.

"You didn't do a good enough job pretending to be wounded. When I tell you to play injured, you play injured. Understand?"

"Yes, sir."

"It may save your life someday. You never know when you might need to play dead. Did anyone get the lesson I was trying to teach you?" The veteran looked around at the shaken men, most still recovering from their recent ordeal. "Anyone?"

Julius stared at his still trembling hands. The instructor looked at him. "Not even you, Caesar?" Julius shook his head.

"It took five of you to carry back one wounded man. I just took six men out of the fight with only one weapon. That, my friends, is effective." He paused, looking at the disheveled men. "Alright, everyone—even you, Recruit Gwendyrn—back on the line. We will practice until you can hit a human target at fifty feet! I'd rather you be on the delivery end of the plumbata, rather than the receiving end."

~ * * * ~

Just a few minutes before lights out, Julius sat on the edge of his bunk, rubbing the new calluses on his hands. His arms ached. His back ached. There was not one part of his body that did *not* ache. He had lost track of the days of the week and even what month it was. He held up the letter from his little sister, a very detailed letter for a seven-year-old that included a picture she had drawn of their family. Marciena wore a dress and held a book; their mom was busy weaving; their father was rebuilding the autodryer. The cartoon Julius, clad in armor and carrying a shield, fought off some nameless, many-armed monster. His sister appeared to have a future as an artist. Laughing, he turned the paper to see it more clearly in the weak light from the gas lantern above his bunk.

In the next bunk, Gwendyrn turned toward him, raising an eyebrow. "What's so funny, Julius?" he drawled. Julius showed him the drawing. "Must be nice to have family around here. I'm the only one in my family who can read, much less write."

"I saved up money for her to go to school. That's where my signing bonus went," Julius confided. "I want her to have a better life than my family. I want her to be able to marry up, maybe become the wife of some merchant or artificer. She'd be a real asset, with her drawing skills. I know my family couldn't pay a dowry, but the way I see it, education ought to be a dowry."

"Do you miss them?" Gwendyrn asked as he handed the drawing back to Julius, who nodded. The other man rolled onto his back and stared up at the ceiling. "I would say that I miss my family too, but I sincerely doubt they miss me. I was too much trouble for them. I ate too much food and got into too many fights with the neighbors. Magistrate finally gave me the choice: prison or the army. Guess I picked the right one. At least here, I get to blow things up." He rubbed at the reddish fuzz growing in on his shaven head.

Julius grabbed his helmet from his open trunk at the foot of his bed. He carefully folded up the letter from his sister and placed it under the lining on the inside of his helmet. He returned the helmet to the trunk, making sure it was in perfect condition before shutting the lid. It wouldn't do for a surprise inspection to find something amiss with his gear.

"Anyone know what new torture they have for us tomorrow?" Recruit Hespinus asked from a few bunks down.

"I heard that we we're finally getting our real equipment. No more of these mock double-weight sword fights. Now we're going to be using the real thing," another man answered.

Julius was excited. Real equipment—they must be getting closer to the end now! They didn't let the complete rejects handle the real weapons. It was too easy to hurt yourself with a failed thrust. He turned so he could see the tribune's room at the end of the barracks. The door was open, and inside, the tribune was having a conversation with Centurion Vibius. Constantine hadn't been around for a few days. *I wonder where he went,* Julius thought.

The centurion walked out of the room and over to a dial on the wall. "Lights out, men," he called out. "Tomorrow is the start of your last month of training. Hopefully, you all make it. Alive." Vibius rotated the dial, and the lights above Julius and the other men winked out.

Julius pulled the sheets up over him, and was asleep in moments. He dreamed of a large, nameless monster chasing him through his dreams, oblivious to all his attempts to stop it.

~ * * * ~

After a breakfast of warm hash and something possibly identifiable as oatmeal, the men of the 13th Cohort filed out of the dining hall with 7th Cohort and drew themselves up on opposite sides of the field, centurions and tribunes in front of them.

Legate General Minnicus rounded the corner of the administration building, trailing aides, and advanced to the middle of the drill ground. Tribune Appius, 7th Cohort Tribune Lominus, and Master Drill Instructor Felix all saluted him. The legionnaires stood at attention.

The general's arm moved up quickly, then slowed into a picture-perfect salute, his iron prosthesis whirring and clicking into position. Components audibly clicked as he slowly lowered it, each part shifting back into place. Looking at each cohort, Minnicus said, "Men, from now on, your two cohorts will be partnered up. You will compete against each other. You will train with each other. After two weeks, there will be a series of tests. How well you do in each test will determine your final assignment and role within our legion.

"As you well know, not every man can be a front line legionnaire! We have need of engineers, quartermasters, rear guards, artillerymen, and skirmishers. A legion is just like a human body. Muscle means nothing if we can't out-think or out-maneuver our opponents."

He paused, sweeping his eyes over each cohort and stopping on the leaders. "Of course, in addition to the results of the trials, outside factors, observations, and the like will be taken into account. I will be making the final decision. May the goddess of victory, Nike, bring you success." He ended with another salute.

Drill Instructor Felix marched out and with a crisp turn, faced the assembled cohorts. He sucked in a deep breath. "Alright, men, we're going to quick-march to the armory, where you will receive your full equipment kits. Then I will spend the day showing you weaklings how to put on all the equipment and how to use it all. And—Jupiter forbid—if you break anything, I will spend all day watching you clean everyone else's equipment with a toothbrush until it is spotless!"

A few sniggers came from the assembled cohorts. The drill instructor glared. "Don't think I didn't see who was laughing. You will be cleaning everyone's equipment and *they* will find it funny. Seventh Cohort, move out!"

Seventh Cohort stepped forward, their tribune pacing his men smartly. Felix waited until the 7th had passed, their boots kicking up a modest dust cloud, before ordering the 13th forward as well. He turned and marched alongside as they marched toward the most grueling, challenging, and strenuous two weeks of their lives.

General Minnicus watched the procession, his dark eyes never leaving the tall tribune of the 13th Cohort. Even after the cohorts had passed out of sight, he remained standing on the field, lost in thought. With a slight shake of his head, he turned back toward his aides.

CHAPTER

6

I T WAS RUSH HOUR IN central Brittenburg's train station and the massive building, more a vault nearly a mile long and almost ten stories high, was bustling. All motortrolley lines in the city converged outside the station, and multiple trains departed and arrived on a strict schedule. Thousands of people walked among the columns, passing or pausing at vendors working the station, either out on the floor or in the restaurants, pubs, shops, and ticket booths set into alcoves in the walls. Most were oblivious to the glory of the ceiling arching high overhead, the frescoes and stained glass windows portraying images of Emperor Caesar III, reigning monarch during the station's completion. What they did pay attention to was the humongous board listing train departures and arrivals along one sidewall, continuously updated by teams of men, or the large clock tower in the center of the terminal.

Corbus wore workingman clothes, neither too shabby nor too fine, but a simple brown, sleeved tunic over coarse canvas pants, and a blue cap pulled down low over his eyes. A dark leather utility belt, faded and cracked with time, completed his disguise. Not that he truly needed one, but it would help if he happened to run into an auxiliary officer.

Avoid standing out not by being invisible, but by being so typical you are uninteresting—he'd taken the words to heart.

He'd allowed the flow and pull of the crowd to guide his movements toward his goal, a small maintenance hatch just behind one of the massive support columns. It had taken him almost half an hour to work his way close to the door, but he'd been in no hurry. Now he stepped close and quickly picked its lock, defeating the basic tumbler in under ten seconds. It clicked open and he scooted inside, gently closing the door behind him. He stood in a barren hallway stretching left and right, wanly lit by overhead lights and currently empty of people in both directions. Pulling a tin badge from a pouch on his belt, he fixed it to his tunic, then consulted the small sign hanging on the wall across from the door, turned, and briskly strode off to the right. *March straight ahead. If you act like you know what you are doing, no one will challenge you, especially armed with this important piece of tin.*

Several times he passed other employees in the hallway though, sure enough, he was ignored. Eventually the hallway widened into a larger area with a series of doors in walls that were scarred and stained with age. Despite its decrepit appearance, the place hummed with activity, with workers, managers, and assistants moving this way and that. Ignoring the cold tingle of sweat on the back of his neck, he grabbed a rolling cart resting against the wall and moved quickly through this area, not wanting his disguise to be called into question. He abandoned the cart when he reached a set of stairs, and began climbing them. Halfway up, he paused and took a deep breath, feeling weak with tension. *You are the instigator of freedom. You are the cloaked hand, the most hidden dagger that strikes without warning. Get it together!* Corbus told himself.

At the top of the stairs he stopped, reading the signs again before turning left. Halfway down the hall, he finally halted in front of a blue door, its paint chipped and faded. A discolored sign on the door read *Secondus Domino Apparatus Gnaevous.* Corbus rapped on the door.

"Come in," called a voice. Corbus entered the room.

A middle-aged administrator was busily writing notes on a massive metal desk. "Just put the reports on a table over there," he said without looking up. "I have to head over to the control room in a minute." When the man did look up, he frowned in confusion. "You aren't Lucius."

"No, not Lucius," Corbus agreed, lifting the miniature crossbow. It twanged, and Domino Gnaevous slumped forward, a needle-sharp bolt piercing his heart. Blood seeped in a dark stain across the papers on his desk.

Corbus hurried around the desk and eased the dead man back in his chair. *Now, where is the key?* He looked through pockets and desk drawers, pulling out massive piles of junk that the thoroughly entrenched bureaucrat seemed to have accumulated everywhere. Finally, he triumphantly held up a chain from which dangled a small pyramid with several grooves and dashes encoded along its flat bottom—the key. *Mission accomplished. The first part, anyway.* Now all he had to do was get to the control room.

Corbus carefully rested Gnaevous's head back on the desk, hoping the dead man would appear to be sleeping, then hastily shoved piles of paper back under the desk, and straightened to scan the room, looking for any minor detail he might have missed. *Good.*

Moving quickly now, he exited the room, pausing only to hang an *Out for lunch* sign on the doorknob. That would delay an alarm only so long before somebody investigated why the murdered man was taking an exceptionally long lunch at ten in the morning. Corbus hoped it would be long enough.

He almost ran now, heading higher and higher up into the building. When an alarm began ringing faintly far below him, he knew he had only minutes. The corridor he was in turned sharply and he pressed himself against the wall to peek around the corner. *Finally!* The control room was just ahead. Corbus pulled a bandana up over the lower half of his face. Although time was precious now, it would all be for naught if someone could identify him later on.

He raced around the corner, down the hall, and pushed the door open so violently, it banged off the wall. He stopped over the threshold and looked at the two large banks of machines, all humming and whirring away, warming the room with their electrical activity: the control center of the entire Brittenburg Central Station complex. Steam lines, fuel lines, electrical lines, water lines—all were controlled from this room. Behind the banks of machines were large windows that overlooked the snarl of train tracks in the yard outside. Although there was only one line into and out of the city, the station could accommodate almost twenty trains at once, and the lines quickly split outside the city.

Several steam and control valve operators working in the room whirled when Corbus burst in, their mouths dropping open in surprise. In an instant, Corbus was among them, delivering a sharp jab to one man's neck, then a tight punch to another operator's gut as he raced down the central aisle. Other operators advanced, scrambling up from their positions.

Brannnnng ... Brannnnnng ... Brannnnnng the main yard alarm blared. Someone had hit an alert switch

"Son of Pluto!" Corbus swore as he continued his dance of death in the control room. Two more men went down, one knocking his head against a panel, the other one eliminated with the quick thrust of a dagger to his neck.

The last three men charged, one brandishing a lamp, the other two wielding a screwdriver and a belt knife. Corbus slid to the right, concealing himself behind a bank of controls. Quick as a striking snake, he tripped the man bearing the lamp, sending him flying down the aisle to land with a thump and a clang as the lamp rolled free. He ducked the screwdriver swung by the man whose nametag identified him as *Ruvius*, then grabbed his arm and bent it sharply back. With a cry, Ruvius crumpled to curl into a ball around his shattered wrist.

One man remained, and he kept his distance, obviously realizing that, the longer he remained functional to keep Corbus from damaging too many critical control valves, the more likely it was that help would arrive. After circling for a moment or two, Corbus ran out of patience. He drew out his miniature crossbow and fired, the bolt lancing across the space between the two men. Seeing the movement, the operator dove out of the way just in time. With his quarry distracted for the moment, Corbus hurdled the control panel between them and hit the man with both feet as he stood up, his opponent's belt knife flashing forward. It scored along his arm, but Corbus's momentum knocked the man hard against the large observation window. Cracks radiated outward, then the window shattered, and the screaming man disappeared from view.

With the last threat eliminated, Corbus checked his bleeding arm. It wasn't serious now, but it would definitely worsen, the longer he left it untreated. He ripped some material from a cloak slung over the back of a chair and tied it around his forearm as best he could to staunch the bleeding. Then he refocused on his mission.

He walked along the bank of controls, frantically searching the identification tags for the one he sought. He paused to close the control room door as he passed, and shoved a chair up under the doorknob. Finally he located the control panel he wanted and began pulling levers down. In the yard, lights began flashing green as tracks were designated "open" for traffic.

After opening every line, Corbus pressed several buttons that triggered green lights outside the station in both the wall tunnel and exterior "wait" stations, where trains idled for their opportunity to enter the city. That done, he set about damaging, destroying, incapacitating, and generally wreaking havoc upon the banks of machines. Sparks flew as he used a found hammer to knock levers out of alignment and break internal gears and gauges, then he cut and ripped out power lines.

At last, drained by the labor, Corbus wiped sweat from his brow and leaned on a windowsill to look out into the yard at the fruit of his endeavors. He grinned. Several trains had all left at the same time, and one had run into another, derailing several passenger cars. One had flipped over, and fire licked up its side. Passengers climbed out of windows, several injured; others appeared trapped. He could hear the distant wail of emergency responders approaching the scene, but it was a squawk from the speaking tube nearby that got his attention.

He lifted the stopper. "Control Room here," he stated calmly.

"This is the mainline switch operator. What in Jupiter's name is going on?" a voice shouted.

Corbus smiled at the fear and panic in the man's voice. "Whatever are you talking about?" he asked sweetly.

"Don't you give me that, sonny," the voice growled. "What is your name and employee number? You'll face the board for this!" the switch operator shouted.

"Too bad I honestly don't care. Enjoy cleaning up your massive problem." Corbus began to replace the stopper in the tube, then thought of an idea. Lifting several paperweights from the table beside the tube, he dropped them one by one down the tube. The tube would look functional, but it would require great effort to clear the blockage.

Confident now that his work was done, Corbus headed for the door, then stopped, hearing heavy footsteps pounding closer out in the hallway. Moments later a resounding crash shook the door, which bent inward slightly under the force of the blow. *Alright, on to Plan B.* He fiddled with his utility belt for a moment, then secured one end of a coil of thin, high tensile rope to a control unit. He tossed the other end out the broken window, cleared the larger shards of glass away with his belt knife, and swung over the sill, hands gripping the rope. As the door burst open under the force of another crash, he was already lowering himself down the rope to freedom. *All this work, and it wasn't even the main event! I wonder how Mom's mission is going?*

~ * * * ~

Amalia and her men had successfully infiltrated the military supply compound on the edge of the main train yard. It had been simple work to eliminate the two bored legionnaires at the front gate, and now her men stood guard in their uniforms. The rest of her small party stuck close to the shadows of the supply warehouse, waiting for the distraction that would pull most of the remaining guards away from the central records room and armory section of the facility.

As alarms began to scream in the distance, Amalia peered around a large stack of wooden crates, watching as several guards lazily picked up their equipment and wandered over in curiosity. A clattering in the office behind them indicated that the telegraph machine was typing out a message. Several moments later, an officer came out of the office and, arms waving, shouted orders. An under-officer quickly formed up a squad and away they marched, double-timing it across the tracks toward the main station.

This was their chance. Amalia silently gathered her team about her and outlined her plan in a whisper. Her second in command, a young ganger named Fustus, took charge of most of the team. Silent as ghosts, they rushed the quartermaster's office. There were a few shouts and some screams during a brief skirmish between the surprised office workers and the ambushers, then silence. A shadow behind the window curtains revealed Fustus as he poked his head out to beckon to her.

He was wiping his sword with a rag as she approached. "Three corrupt workers dead; one of ours got unlucky in the exchange." He gestured to the long, gawky body of a ganger lying on the floor. The young man's eyes were open, still looking surprised at the foot of steel that had been thrust through his stomach to sever his spine. The legionary who had been quick enough to draw his weapon to inflict the death blow was dying as well, bleeding out from several stab wounds a few feet away from the dead ganger.

"Bring his body," Amalia ordered. "We don't want anyone to know who we are, or even that there was more than one of us. Get the men busy loading up all the supplies we can carry. Also, take those uniforms off the dead men. We can clean off some of the blood. They may be useful."

At that moment, a series of piercing squeals and explosions shook the building as several trains crashed into each other, and the flames from one ignited the cargo of another. Several of her followers gave a cheer. "Shush! We don't want to draw attention to ourselves!" Amalia snapped, and got them focused on the task of liberating as much as possible from the supply depot. Inwardly, she smiled— Corbus must have been successful. But where was he? He should have been here a while ago to rendezvous for the return to their safe houses.

"Domina! A strange man is running toward us from the terminal!" a gang lookout hissed as he aimed his repeating crossbow at the running figure. "Should I take him down?"

Amalia trained her binoculars on the running man. Although he was cloaked and a bandana covered half his face, Amalia would recognize that lope anywhere. She waved off the lookout. "Don't shoot; it's Corbus, making his late entrance, as usual," she said with an unrestrained grin. She had spent years training him in all the deadly arts that she knew, and one day, he would take over her position and lead their people to independence and victory.

Behind her, men were gathering as many boxes of armor, rations, explosive warheads, artillery components, and other supplies as their vehicle could handle. A man with a can of black paint quickly brushed over the black eagle icons on the side of each box to help disguise the origin. Corbus ran up just as they were loading the last of the boxes onto the six-legged transport hauler, one of hundreds in the city. The rest of her party scrambled inside, two men carrying the ganger's body. The nondescript vehicle would attract no notice as long as her crew appeared calm.

Seeing the bloodied cloth on his arm, Amalia frowned as she looked her son up and down. "What happened? Someone get lucky with a crossbow bolt?"

"No, someone got close with a belt knife. Don't worry, I repaid the favor with a five-story drop," Corbus quipped. His tight smile never reached his eyes, but still Amalia laughed. The cold, manic laughter floated through the cavernous warehouse.

Fustus beckoned to them from the walker's control shack, and Corbus and Amalia walked toward the hauler. Amalia pulled an explosive plumbata warhead from her belt. She turned and threw it into a nearby stack of military gear. The explosion was impressive, and several boxes caught fire. "That will keep their attention for a while," she said as she turned and entered the hauler. With a whine, the hauler's steam boiler powered up and the six legs moved it steadily away from the scene. They didn't want to be anywhere near the warehouse when forty tons of military grade supplies, including black powder, erupted.

It was one of the last vehicles to pass through an auxilia cordon before it closed, a few blocks away. Behind them, the auxiliary were searching vehicles and checking permits. It was too little, too late.

Amalia and Corbus both stayed belowdecks to avoid attention as a cool Fustus guided the hauler through the streets, monitoring their movement carefully to prevent any of the material in the hold from shifting and crushing his friends and leaders. A gut-wrenching hour later, he steered the vehicle carefully into the loading dock of an abandoned warehouse in Sludge Bottom, locked the legs in place, removed the key, and powered down the boilers to prevent damage to the pipes that fed the steam to the power turbine. He climbed down the access ladder into the hold and helped supervise the unloading process.

Amalia and Corbus met him at outside. "Excellent job, storming the quartermaster's office, Fustus," Amalia said, impressed by the man's quick thinking in the warehouse and his professional actions and responses to her questions. "I've been discussing with Corbus a brainstorm I had—a way to wreak more havoc upon those poor, incompetent overlords of ours. We both thought you would be the best man for the job."

Nearby, Corbus idly picked at his fingernails with his knife. "I still think he'll be in over his head," he said. "He's barely begun to shave."

Fustus's face turned red, but he held his tongue. Amalia smiled. It wasn't smart to insult arguably the best assassin and death-dealer in the rebel ranks, and Fustus had kept his wits about him, maintaining his casual stance. Fustus's eyes did bore into Corbus's, though. Eventually her son blinked, shrugged nonchalantly, and turned away.

Amalia watched as Fustus, now pale, let out a slow breath. "See, dear, I told you he could handle the pressure," she cooed. "Now Fustus, I was thinking about something big involving those new uniforms we ... procured ... today." Turning, she gestured for Fustus to walk with her and they moved off, he nodding agreement to her plans.

CHAPTER

7

C ONSTANTINE TURNED ASIDE THE INCOMING blow with a teeth-clenching screech and a shower of sparks as the two swords' electrical charges connected. He stood face to face with his opponent, one of the biggest men in 7th Cohort. Weary now, they did little more than jostle, and Constantine took the moment to look around. His men had fallen back into a rough circle, the "uninjured" men creating a wall with their shields facing outward. "Injured" men lay on the ground, many stunned from the low electrical shocks of the practice swords.

A high tweet sounded and Constantine's opponent backed toward his men, the two sides resting as the 7th Cohort reformed. Constantine checked his equipment and looked at his men. Recruits Caesar , Hespinus, Gwendyrn, and four others stood in a tight knot. Vibius stood next to him, panting.

"We've fought well, sir, but they're just bigger and have longer reach. They broke our formation with that flying wedge, and we couldn't reform. As they say, sir, it's all but over."

Constantine looked around again. His men were haggard and tired, but they still held onto their weapons. He raised his voice. "I don't think I've said this much, men, but it's truly been an honor to lead you. We have come a long way together. Remember, this fight determines our assignment in this legion. So I have one last question for you." He paused, and his men looked at him quizzically. "Do. You. Want. To. Be. Cooks?" He shouted the last word from a hoarse throat.

Grinning wolfishly, they shouted in unison, "No, SIR!"

Constantine smiled.

"I don't know about you, sir, but my ma always said my *garum* was fit to kill a man. Or a beast," Gwendyrn added. "I don't think I'd like being brought up for treason on account I poisoned the entire legion." The fermented fish sauce was considered a Roman staple. It was perhaps the only industry not allowed back inside the city limits even after several hundred years.

"Then we'd better not subject them to your cooking, Gwendyrn. Men, if we are going to go down, then at least let's give them a beating they won't soon forget!" The men gave a ragged cheer. A few checked their shield straps. "We'll give them everything we've got," Constantine said, watching the remnants of 7th Cohort advancing toward them. "Ready, men, on my mark."

Seventh's dented blue shields formed a moving wall. "Ready," Constantine whispered, only slight movements and tensing legs betraying his soldiers' preparations. "Charge!"

As one, the 13th Cohort ran forward, swords raised, screaming at the top of their lungs. Constantine formed the point of their flying wedge. The clash was tremendous. Gwendyrn used his shield like a battering ram to crush an opposing soldier, then whirled with his sword, zapping one, two, then three soldiers, pushing aside their weapons with brute strength.

Julius raced to cover his furious assault, blocking sword swings from other 7th Cohort members. A thwack on the back of his legs made his body convulse. His eyes rolled back and he dropped. Seconds later, Gwendyrn's limp body fell atop his as he succumbed to the blows of five other men.

Vibius and Constantine were fighting back to back, fending off blows and striking back as best they could. The last of the 13th Cohort legionnaires fell to their left, outnumbered three to one. Vibius barely managed to raise his shield in time as a sword whipped over the top and hit him on the side of his helmet. Rattled, his defense wavered and he went down a split second later. Constantine, desperate now, went on a furious charge, knocking down three opposing legionnaires with well-timed sword strokes, but even his training by the elite Emperor's Praetorian Guard couldn't help him when outnumbered ten to one. His muscles burned and his vision swam as, at last, he was brought to his knees under a flurry of shocks and blunt sword strikes.

In the background, another whistle blew. The 7th Cohort men stood panting, as medics and orderlies rushed onto the field to take the injured men off and return them to their quarters. Constantine looked at the state of each cohort and saw how close it had been. Seventh Cohort had barely ten men left standing, all with minor injuries and a few shaking off close hits from the specially-made shock training swords.

An orderly helped Constantine stand. His legs felt like jelly and he fought down the sharp taste of bile in his mouth. He would not throw up in front of his men. He would not embarrass them in that manner.

General Minnicus was approaching. Constantine tried to stand at attention, but his legs would not support him. He counted himself lucky that he was still able to salute.

Minnicus returned his salute. "May I congratulate you, Tribune? That was a fine showing indeed. Your men fought to the last, and that was admirable. Well led and well controlled. Shame you couldn't pull it out in the end, but quantity has a quality all its own." Minnicus smiled a knowing smile.

"Thank you, sir, but I believe you should be congratulating 7th Cohort; they won fair and square. They broke our formation and split us in two." Constantine's brain was still fuzzy, but he could sense there was something else Minnicus was getting at.

"Yes, and even though they were separated, your men fought well and managed to get back to you. Your sub-units were capable and motivated even in your absence. Even down to the last, bitter moments." Minnicus looked at a drill instructor over on the reviewing stand. The man nodded and Minnicus's eyebrow rose. "It seems we are in a bit of a quandary here. You see, Tribune, we already have enough front line cohorts, as well as reserve cohorts. We also have an excellent engineering cohort, quartermaster cohort, several skirmish and artillery cohorts, and frankly, we don't need another Mess cohort. So we weren't sure what to do with you." Minnicus looked at his notebook, and gestured to an aide. They held a low conversation, the aide nodding and writing furiously.

Constantine's heart sank. His father's last words before he left were, *Don't mess this up.* He felt as though he had failed his men. They would now be relegated to fort building duty or maybe even baggage and logistics. It was unfathomable. He had failed.

Minnicus turned back around. "But I have an idea. One that I think will revolutionize this army and force those petulant, pudgy, idiots in top hats and senatorial capes south of the Tiber to pay attention. I'm stealing an idea from the Nortlanders and assigning your cohort the position of *vis volatilis incursio*, or Rapid Assault Force. I'll figure out your job specifics later, but in the meantime, it looks like you'll be able to avoid latrine-digging duty."

Minnicus leaned closer so that only Constantine could hear. "Besides, no one would dare try to remove you from a position, with your family connections." He winked at the startled tribune, then straightened. "Take the rest of the day off, Tribune. You and your men get some rest. We'll have a meeting tomorrow morning. I'll send a messenger to confirm the time." Minnicus saluted.

Wearily, Constantine returned the salute. In the blink of an eye, the fortunes of his cohort had been reversed. Now they were the first of their kind in the Roman army, a rapid assault force, whatever that meant. Constantine was sure that, after today, nothing would faze him or his men. It looked like lucky Cohort 13 was still at the top of their game.

~ * * * ~

In retrospect, Constantine thought, he should never have tempted the Fates in that manner. This was definitely the most terrifying experience of his life. Yes, he had ridden in a dirigible before, even the sleek, rakish-looking military versions. But why would he want to jump out of a perfectly good airship? It made absolutely no sense.

"So the idea is, sir, we use the ship to get behind the enemy, then drop you guys off with the idea of making mischief or setting up a position that forces them to divert a maximum amount of soldiers, thus allowing the rest of the legion to be victorious. We support you with heavier weaponry from above, and you hold the line, build a quick fort, and hold out for backup," a junior aviator was explaining. The Rapid Assault Force would quickly strike behind enemy lines, causing as much damage as possible by disrupting operations, stalling reinforcements, and interrupting communications before withdrawing with only a few minutes' notice.

"I have no problem with all of that," Constantine said. "But I do have two concerns. First, how will we be evacuated, or are we expected to simply stand around, be surrounded, and die? Second, why in Jupiter's name do we have to jump out of a perfectly good airship? Couldn't it simply land and let us out? I'd much prefer that option."

The airman smiled and let out a shallow laugh. "You may prefer that, sir, but I guarantee you, we aviators would not enjoy it. Our gasbag is a pretty nice, inviting target. Also, do you plan on giving the enemy a chance to reinforce an area before you have a chance to do something about it? We won't be sitting ducks."

He motioned to a small planning table in the middle of the vessel. The men and officers crowded around it. He activated a switch underneath. A low hum permeated the air and the table seemed to come to life, its surface rippling into contours and small hills, valleys, and other miniature geographical features.

"This is a Mark II command table. It uses magnets and steam power to create a physical map of the terrain, input from that standard topographical map." The aviator's gloved hand pointed to a palm-sized map being fed into the machine's control panel, bumps and grooves indicating map features. "This will give us visual knowledge of the terrain that would be the best to screen our movements for hit-and-run tactics. Instead of landing, your men will perform a slide-drop onto an objective, or as near to it as we can manage. The ropes will be used to lift your men up as well as lower them. You'll be using lockable *carpteneo* mechanisms to slow and stop your descent individually. They are the best version to date, and have a success rate of 98%. I've used them myself many times. It's how we would evacuate this beauty, should the need ever arise. Any other questions?"

Constantine looked up from the command table. His men all wore expressions of nervous apprehension. Even the steadfast Centurion Vibius was looking green. "Well, men," he said, "are you ready to see if a legionnaire can learn to fly as well as he can learn to fight?"

"Sir, *yes sir!*" the men answered.

"Any man who wishes to back out now will not suffer any repudiation or punishment. I'll gladly transfer you to another cohort in the legion. This is your chance—once we're up in the air, you're coming down the hard way with the rest of us."

For a moment no one moved. There was a slight shuffle as heads turned to stare at their neighbors.

"Alright then, Airman Souzetio, what next?"

The aviator pulled the plug out of a speaking tube and shouted an order into it. Almost immediately, Constantine felt a rumble toward the back of the ship. The men crowded to the windows. For many of them, this was their first time aboard an airship. The slight jostle and the increasing angle of the floor indicated that the dirigible was indeed airborne.

On the catwalk surrounding the oblong gondola, several crewmembers were throwing off lines. A brief, shouted command brought several together at a nearby winch. Together, the men began rotating the winch faster and faster. A telescoping spindle shot out from below the deck. One of the men, watching a small gauge, held up a hand. The other men stopped the winch. They secured it and dispersed. The senior deckhand adjusted a series of brass levers until large white sails slid from the side-mast.

"They help with adjusting altitude." Souzetio had appeared at Constantine's side. "We can adjust the ballast or helium amount for large altitude adjustments, but it's easier to simply use sails and the rudder to make minute changes to our course."

Constantine nodded, impressed by the technological know-how behind the side sails. He discussed the technology with Souzetio for a bit, getting a feel for the man who would be their primary contact person with the air fleet.

"Is there any way I can visit the bridge? I'd like to meet the captain and introduce myself."

The airman nodded. "Certainly, sir. Right this way." The man led him to a hatch in the bulkhead and slid the door aside. They continued through several other compartments, each one holding different systems critical to their continued ability to stay in the air. Constantine saw the engine room, a storage room, a weapons bay, small crew bunkroom, and a tiny galley. Finally they approached a wood-paneled door that appeared elegant compared to the exposed steel beams and bolts around it.

"This is the bridge, Tribune Appius. Please give me a moment to ensure that this is an acceptable time to observe." Airman Souzetio knocked on the door and entered, clicking the door quietly shut behind him.

Constantine took a moment to examine the map of the ship that was bolted to the wall, tracing his finger along the central corridor that ran like a spine down the middle of the gondola. The gondola's upper level held the living quarters, engineering rooms, and storage areas, while most of the weapons bays were on the bottom level. *That makes sense,* Constantine thought. Obviously, if they couldn't see the targets below, they couldn't shoot at them.

His finger traced the open lower level deck, where his men would descend, precariously strung out along hundreds of feet of wire. There were open deck areas on both levels at the back of the ship, meaning a total of ten lines could theoretically be dropped and manned. *It will be like falling ...*

Pushing that thought gruffly from his mind, Constantine let his hand fall to his side, and waited. But a distant memory thrust itself into his consciousness.

~ * * * ~

"Hurry up, Constantine, you're going too slow!" came Lucius' high-pitched call.

That was Lucius, always trying to show off how big and strong he was compared to me. I was seven!

Constantine looked around at the branches supporting his weight, then tipped his head back to see his brother. Lucius was waiting on one of the highest branches of one of the tallest maple trees in the palace gardens.

"I can see the Air Fleet from up here!" Lucius crowed, trying to coax his younger brother higher.

I should have known something was off that day. Constantine and his older brother had never been real playmates. Nor had they ever been very close, even as brothers. Rather, they *coexisted* ... and, occasionally, interacted in the manner that children do. That is to say, Lucius got into trouble with Constantine and blamed it on his younger brother. *That day was no different.*

Constantine looked hesitantly up at the next level of branches. "It's too high!" he called back, unable to keep a thread of fear out of his voice. "I can see just fine from here," he added, the lie thin and obvious. *Lucius could always see through my lies, especially when I was afraid.*

Lucius climbed down several branches. His grin was malevolent. *How could an eleven-year-old have such a smile?*

"You aren't afraid of heights now, are you?" Constantine shook his head, alarmed. "You've been on airship flights before; this is no different." Lucius dropped to stand next to him on the same solid branch, grasping a nearby limb for support.

"It is very different," Constantine replied. *An airship is metal and steel and glass and you can feel it under you,* the tribune Constantine thought again, just as he had then. *You know when it will go up or down. On a tree, if you fall, that's it.* "On an airship, I can pretend that I'm simply on a boat." *I should never have said that last part aloud.*

"What? Stop talking nonsense." Lucius exclaimed. His lips tightened. "You're afraid of climbing a tree? You'd rather ride boats?" He pushed against the branch he grasped, pushing the limb they were standing on up and down.

The swaying made Constantine's heart race faster, and he cried out.

"Little brother is scared of a little rocking?" Lucius sniffed. "You can't be an emperor if you get scared. That's why I'm the heir."

The limb Lucius was pushing against suddenly snapped. Overbalanced, Lucius fell backward, arms flailing, and fell the fifteen feet to the ground. Hands tight on the tree's trunk, Constantine shouted his horror, watching helplessly.

Lucius landed with a thud and writhed slowly on the ground. Servants and guards rushed to his aid. Their tutor turned his wizened eyes up to Constantine and crooked his finger in an unmistakable *come here* gesture.

He never forgave me for that perceived insult, Constantine thought as the memory faded. *He never would believe that he was the one who broke the branch, that I had not plotted to embarrass him. What was it like even then, the pressure of being heir, or knowing that if he wasn't good enough, father could appoint me instead? Well, that pressure's not on me; Lucius has been fully groomed, and I'm the younger son, shipped off to the army. I just have to jump out of a dirigible.*

~ * * * ~

The door opened and a deck rating poked his head out. "Please come in, Tribune."

Constantine nodded his thanks and walked through the door. The front third of the top deck was given over to the bridge, and the view through the large observation windows, angled to allow for maximum visibility, was incredible. Observation bubbles popped out on both sides of the bridge, providing an even greater viewing range. Within the bridge, several crewmembers monitored a central bank of levers, dials, and gauges, occasionally making tiny adjustments to the controls. The officer of the watch monitored their efforts, and another officer stood in one of the observation bubbles, intent on the view to port. A single security officer stood against the wall to the right.

Airman Souzetio stood next to a leather-backed command chair bolted to a platform in the middle of the deck. A bronze speaking tube came out of the ceiling and ended right around head height next to the chair. Straightening his back, Tribune Appius marched toward the chair.

"Ah, there you are, Tribune. I was wondering when we might be getting a visit from you," the officer in the observation bubble said as he passed. Constantine stopped and saluted. The ship captain gave a half-salute response, offending Constantine's sense of protocol. As officers of essentially similar rank, he had expected an equally crisp salute acknowledging this.

Seeing the look on his face, the captain barked a short laugh. "You'll find we aren't quite as stiff and formal as the legions, Tribune. You'll get our respect when you earn it. In the meantime, there is far too much to do to waste all our time saluting each other in the proper increment." His tone was terse, and Constantine couldn't help but feel mollified and a bit abashed. The man gestured. "Come over here and see where we are. I'll describe the plan to you. I assume that Suzzy's gone over the plan with you?" At Constantine's blank look, he added, "Excuse me, I meant Airman Souzetio."

"Yes he did, Captain ..."

"Oh for Jupiter's sake, I forgot to introduce myself. I'm so busy rambling on about the mission that I plum overlooked that. Captain Tiveri Rufius Alexandros, of His Majesty's Airship *Scioparto,* at your service." Both of the captain's calloused hands enveloped Constantine's hand and he shook it firmly, his expression enthusiastic. Constantine found himself warming to the seemingly eccentric captain.

"So, Captain Alexandros, how did you end up with this job? I can't imagine many ship captains would be willing to leave their ship motionless over a battlefield to drop a cohort of men behind enemy lines." The question had been boring a hole in Constantine's brain for several hours now.

"To tell you the truth, I volunteered at the ... *request* ... of General Minnicus. I was the only *volunteer*. No one else wanted to try this new way of fighting a war. But I think it will be a great 'Emperor card up the sleeves' of our legion, if you know what I mean. I want to be remembered for helping start this revolution of thinking."

Constantine found himself appreciating the captain even more. He was risking not just his life, but also his ship and the lives of his crew, as well as his career. He even genuinely seemed to care about them. Constantine always believed that you could tell something about a man by the way he treated his workers. He didn't consider himself a man of the plebeian class, far from it, but he did believe that men were men, not cogs in a machine, or animals.

Captain Alexandros turned the conversation back to the current situation. "We aim to begin practice here, on these fields east of the fort." He gestured to another command map, where large flat rectangles marked wheat fields. "We'll start by maintaining a position just over fifteen feet off the ground. You'll get your first taste of rope drop there. We'll gradually increase it. It's also an opportunity for my men to practice hauling your soldiers back aboard. That's going to be a new skill for us. Fleet regulations only ever explained evacuation, not embarkation by rope-winch."

Constantine raised his eyebrows at the captain. "You aren't inventing this procedure now, are you?"

The captain shook his head. "No, just performing this highly theoretical action for the first time with live people. We did try it with a bag of flour last week."

Constantine had a sinking feeling he knew what was coming next.

"We ended up dusting the flowers with flour! Ha! Good one, eh? Well, not for our pretend person, but pretty looking, I suppose."

Sighing, Constantine moved to examine the terrain. To his untrained eye, it appeared to be a nice flat practice area. He asked about weather and wind currents.

"Very little to speak of today. I'll drop a few crewmembers down and we can set the anchor down, as well. That'll help prevent our floating away," Alexandros responded cheerfully.

He checked a spinning timepiece on the main control panel. It was mounted on several moving disks that allowed it to stay flat and readable during altitude changes and any other movement. The glistening brass shone in the sunlight filling the bridge. Seeing him squinting, two crewmembers pulled down thin, translucent sunshades, taking the worst blast off the sun's rays. "I estimate about twenty minutes until our arrival. Better go prepare your men.

"Don't be a stranger, Tribune!" he added as Constantine nodded and made to leave. "My door is always open. Figuratively, of course, so please knock before you enter. By the by, would you do me the honor of dining with me tonight after our little escapade? I can truly say I'll be rightly famished by the time we're done."

Constantine hadn't been able to leave the base at all during his basic training periods, so he readily agreed. They made plans to meet later outside the main dining hall, where they would dine with the officers, rather than the enlisted men. Tradition held that new cohorts always ate together during training, officers included. With training done, the separation of ranks promptly began.

With their business concluded, the men saluted each other. Constantine noted with pleasure that the captain's salute was much crisper this time. "May the gods be with you, Tribune, and with your men. Especially the wind gods— pray for gentle winds."

Constantine nodded once, then did an about-face and marched from the bridge, Airman Souzetio trailing him.

~ * * * ~

Julius gripped his carpteneo tightly. The foot-long mechanism weighed about three pounds and had an opening where the rope came in from the top and another opening where it exited the bottom. Side grips could apply pressure to the rope to slow his descent. It could be controlled with just one hand, but Julius did not plan to take any chances. *I'm definitely using two hands on this.*

Just a second ago, he had watched a junior flight officer attach his carpteneo to the line, an audible *click-click* signaling that both hooks had latched securely to the harness around his thighs and waist. The man walked backward right off the edge of the ship and was instantly gone, rapidly sliding down the rope. Everyone who was in a position to watch had leaned over the side of the ship, watching the midshipman swing in the breeze until finally touching down. He unlatched himself and pounded a metal loop into the ground. Pushing the rope through, he pulled it as taut as possible against the resistance of the airship gently bobbing in the wind.

The same wind billowed Airman Souzetio's leather jacket. He had left it unzipped, as they were less than fifty feet above the ground, and the warm breeze was pleasant. He was instructing Julius's group. The rest of the 13th Cohort was split among the three other airdrop positions at the stern of the airship. The two levels of open decking allowed for several drop points. Julius's group was on the port side of A Deck, the lowest level of the ship.

"Alright, lads, this is your first real chance to show what you've learned. Remember, when you first get off the ship, it's okay to go a bit slow. Don't lose your head. Breathe! Loosen your hand, count to two, squeeze, and repeat. That will get you down the rope nice and steady. If this were a real combat drop, you'd be dropping straight down most of the way to avoid any skillful ambusher, while we get to be honking great stationary targets." He looked around. "Alright you men, who is going to be the first to test the Fates?"

Several men shuffled. Julius almost raised his hand, then turned the movement into a nervous arm rub. *Even I'm not quite ready to be the first.*

Tribune Appius spoke from the back of the group. "If you weaklings won't volunteer, then I will take the lead." He pushed his way to the front. "After all, you've got to see how a *real* man does this."

He patiently allowed the airman to take him through the steps again, even though they all understood the routine by heart.

"Clamp your carpteneo to the rope. Make sure the rope is going the right way so you won't be stuck *speeding up* instead of slowing down!" Several laughs escaped from the tight, nervous lips of those in his training group.

"Attach your carpteneo to your harness—make sure you hear the clicks. Then you approach the deck edge, and place your feet on the edge like so." He guided Constantine to the edge of the deck until he now stood at a forty-five degree angle, back toward the empty air, hands tightly squeezing the carpteneo. It was the only thing keeping him anchored to the ship. "Ah, one last thing. Put your goggles on so that you can actually see the ground coming up at you! It would not do for us to have to scrape you off the ground with a spatula."

"Mister Souzetio," the tribune said, "my hands are currently occupied, could you ... ?"

The airman gently pulled the lightweight flying goggles from the metal helmet on Constantine's head down over his eyes. He spent a few seconds adjusting them.

"Thank you, Mister Souzetio. And now, one last word." Constantine looked around, and smiled thinly. "I'll see you on the ground. Last man down runs extra laps tonight." With that, Constantine pushed off hard, flying backward into space.

Julius looked over the rail and saw him following the *squeeze, wait, release, and repeat* steps. The tribune looked like a spider that was lowering herself down a strand of web: dropping, then evaluating, then dropping again. Less than a minute later, Tribune Appius was on the ground, waving at them in an unmistakable *Come here* gesture.

The rest of the training squad lined up to descend the rope. Julius found himself third in line, behind Recruit Gnacius and Recruit Kavalinus. A tap on his shoulder prompted Julius to turn to see Gwendyrn smiling grimly.

"If you stop, I'm not. You'll just be dead, city boy." Gwendyrn's laugh was hard. "I plan on getting down as fast as possible without breaking any body part."

Julius frowned. He had been planning on taking it nice and slow, but with Gwendyrn behind him, he would have to speed up the pace.

Recruit Gnacius latched himself onto the cable and, under Souzetio's coaching, approached the edge. Finally, with a half-terrified, half-croaked, "Hoo*rah!*" he thrust himself out into space. The rope went taut as it bore his weight, but there was no indication of stress. At least that was what it seemed like to Julius, who was nervously watching for any indication of malfunction in his or the ship's equipment.

Gwendyrn caught Julius's expression. "Are you nervous? Are you afraid of dying? There are a lot more things that you're better off worrying about. Look at it this way—if your equipment fails, not only will your family be able to get your death benefit, but your short life will end quickly and with little pain. Many others would be jealous!" His orange mustache quivered, then he nearly doubled over in laughter.

Julius smacked him on the shoulder. *Does he take these horrible lines from a book somewhere? No, Gwendyrn would never stoop to actually* reading *a book.* Aloud he growled, "Shut up before I 'accidentally' cut your harness strap."

Recruit Kavalinus went over the side, still muttering a prayer to Jupiter.

"Keep on moving. We don't have all day!" Airman Souzetio motioned for Julius to move up. Julius swallowed the lump in his throat and shuffled ahead.

Souzetio helped him latch his carpteneo onto the main line. The man's brown eyes found his. He nodded. "You can do this. Don't doubt yourself. Just follow your training. It's the best feeling in the world, after this first go. This one is all about getting rid of the nerves. Next one is all enjoyment," he murmured reassuringly.

"Good luck, don't make a big splotch for me to land in!" called Gwendyrn.

Cold sweat trickled down Julius's back. He could feel it under his helmet and armor. His trembling hands pulled his brass-rimmed goggles over his eyes, then grasped his carpteneo. He inched his way back toward the edge. Souzetio was smiling and waving him ahead. He smile seemed to say, *Hurry up before we die of old age.*

Julius took a deep breath and leaned back into space. *You can do it!* one part of his brain encouraged. *Are you crazy?* the rational part of his brain countered. *Shut up,* he told them both. He bent his knees, and—pushed!

For a moment, it felt as though his stomach had dropped out of his body. The wind whistled past him, twisting him around on the rope. *Remember your training!* His brain screamed at him. Julius grasped the carpteneo with both hands and squeezed. His descent stopped. He continued spinning lazily, getting a panoramic view of the landing field and surrounding forests. Taking a deep breath, Julius loosened his grip on the carpteneo. His body began to creep down the line. A slow smile spread over his face. More confident now, he loosened his grip and his body dropped at a steadier pace.

He briefly looked up and saw Gwendyrn leaning over the side. He appeared to be shaking his head at someone behind him. Focusing on his own situation, Julius continued to tighten, then relax his grip on the line. The ground approached in fits and spurts. Finally, Julius lowered himself the last couple of feet and he gasped out a pent breath as he felt his feet touch *terra firma*. His legs were wobbly and his shaking fingers fumbled as he tried to detach his carpteneo from the line. The ground crew member stepped forward and wordlessly helped.

His knees still weak with the aftermath of terror, Julius hobbled over to the legionaries who had already descended.

Tribune Appius slapped him solidly on the back. "By the gods, Julius, stop making us look like amateurs out there! You'll have to give us all some specialized instruction, it appears!"

The tribune must have nerves of steel, Julius thought as he bent to massage his still trembling legs. *He's even smiling and walking around as if he's on holiday in the Mediterranean.* Only later would Julius learn that the tribune had puked his guts out immediately after landing.

A muffled shout from above drew Julius's eyes upward. Gwendyrn was flailing and spinning on the rope above their heads.

"By Jupiter, the man's gone and lost his head!" cried the deckhand holding the rope. "Quick, help me lower him before he breaks his carpteneo!" Following the tribune's lead, Julius and his companions rushed to grab the rope. With the deckhand chanting the pace, they laboriously pulled the rope down. Men from the other landing ropes ran over to help.

The man above them seemed to float between ship and earth. Julius tilted his head up and released his grip on the rope long enough to undo the strap under his chin and gently toss his helmet behind him. A shiver ran through him as cool air flowed over his shaven scalp. This was taking forever. The men around him were all blinking sweat from their eyes.

Then he had an idea. "Hey, Gwendyrn, you big baby!" he shouted. "Stop throwing a temper tantrum and get your behind in motion! Relax your hands!"

The tribune looked at him, grinned, and cupped his hands around his mouth to add his call to Julius's. "Legionnaire Gwendyrn, if you are not down here in one minute, I am confiscating your beer ration for the rest of the month! *And I will give it to your squadmates!*"

Gwendyrn seemed to pause in his frantic thrashing. Julius shielded his eyes with his hand. Yes! He seemed to be furiously working at the carpteneo in his hands. Finally, he began to slide down the rope again. The men on the ground cheered. When he eventually touched down, his face was tear-streaked and his arms were white with tension. "No one takes my beer from me," he proclaimed.

A few men laughed, but otherwise they exchanged no words. They didn't have to. They were simply glad Gwendyrn was alive and healthy on the ground. Tribune Appius gave the man a clap on the back, then they all moved away, watching the next man descend the thin, tenuous line between the floating warship and the safety of the ground.

The rest of the exercise went without incident. Each group had a few men who had a troublesome first descent, but that was to be expected. When everyone was down, Tribune Appius gathered them all around a convenient stump and stepped up onto it. Facing his men, he removed his red horsehair-crested helmet off his head and tucked it under one elbow.

"Great job with the first descent," he told them. "Unfortunately, if this was a real combat descent, Mister Horatio over here informs me that half of us would be dead, leaving the other half probably fighting for our lives here on the ground, unable to get back up to the ship and safety. Therefore, we shall continue to practice until we can get down in less than five minutes. In addition, gentlemen, we will now practice ascending to the ship. This maneuver is a bit ... rougher ... than your descent was, I'm told."

Julius sighed with several others. Mutters of protest ran through the assembled men.

"Come now, I've heard they've got hot drinks up on the ship as a pick-me-up for our first drop mission together! Of course, last one there may not get any. So line up at your respective wires, and let's show those flyboys that we know our business."

The men shuffled off to their lines. A few minutes later, Julius was being winched back onto the *Scioparto* at a brisk pace. A pair of deckhands waiting by the opening in the railing pulled him back onto the ship. Captain Alexandros himself was there to witness their performance, and Julius realized that this must be a learning experience for him and his men as well. Never before in the history of the Roman Empire had the legions and the air fleet worked so closely together. They were breaking new ground. Julius's chest swelled with pride.

~ * * * ~

At last, Tribune Appius clambered aboard. Naturally, he had been the first man down and the last man off the ground. The captain nodded approvingly. Although he didn't know the tribune that well, he appeared to be a decent sort. Of course, his heritage practically ensured that he would be capable in some way. It was better to be capable in leadership than capable in something less fortunate, such as basket weaving, Alexandros mused as his hand whipped up in a crisp salute. Tribune Appius returned it.

"Welcome back to the ship, Tribune. Glad to have you back safe and sound. If you have the time, I think we should meet on the bridge to discuss how we can modify and improve our deployment next time."

The tribune quickly agreed. As he moved off to give instructions to his senior centurion, Alexandros wondered for the thousandth time that day what quirk of fate had entrusted him to work with a member of the royal family, given that his ancestors had been the ringleaders in an attempt to murder Constantine's ancestor in 33 BC. *Who at the Bureau of State messed this one up?* It mattered naught, for his efforts with this man would give Alexandros and his family a glorious return to the annals of history.

CHAPTER

8

GREGIAS, VALET TO THE EMPEROR Hadrian Silenius Appius, tiptoed around him this morning, and His Royal Highness knew it was because he was in a foul mood. First, he was unable to spend time on his new dirigible, the *Marelena*, due to some technical problems. Second, those cursed *reporters* had run unflattering drawings and stories about him and his heir, Lucius, so Emperor Hadrian was, naturally, upset. Which meant, third, his household irritated him by tiptoeing around him. Hadrian hated those vicious, smelly, untruthful men.

He had considered sending another law to the Senate that made it legal to bring complaints against journalists who wrote untruths about a person. Every time he tried, though, the Senate protested that people had the right to free speech. Of course he could just institute it as a law himself, but that would bring him into conflict with not just the Senate, but the Plebeian Council. They currently happened to be some of his strongest supporters, acting as a useful counterweight to the temperate nature of the Senate.

"Gregias, my third best toga, please," the emperor drawled. "We have decided to view the grounds. We wish to see the *Marelena* during its test flight."

He allowed his valet to drape the heavy robe over his shoulders, securing it around his waist with a broad clockwork-patterned belt. *Autumn in Rome is splendid, especially if you have access to such lovely gardens,* he thought in anticipation. Hadrian suffered through most of the other seasons with the rest of his people who were unable to escape the city—except for winter, and possibly the worst days of summer, and the rainy days of spring. He was not too accepting of hardship.

Several servants, their eyes suitably downcast, proffered trays of delicacies and light snacks. Hadrian delicately selected one sweet almond morsel and popped it into his mouth. He chewed and nodded appreciatively, then snapped his hand out. Another servant waiting patiently on the sidelines stepped forward and deposited a wine glass in the outstretched hand. He took a long sip of heavy red wine to wash the nutty aftertaste from his mouth, smacked his lips, and let the empty goblet fall to the floor. The servant hurried to pick up the bejeweled vessel as Hadrian strode from the room, trailed by the usual cortege of servants, guards, and aides.

Several richly decorated hallways later, a set of double doors swung aside under the hands of two elite Praetorian Guardsmen, their scarlet cloaks spotless, steel breastplates gleaming. The emperor gave them a curt nod as he strode past, stepping into the welcome solitude of a perfectly manicured garden. A pathway took him past flowerbeds and topiaries to a raised pavilion fondly called the Tower, a simple balustraded marble block reached via a single staircase in the back. From here, the emperor could see most of the capital.

Careful to sweep the hem of his heavy toga aside, Hadrian climbed the stairs, paused to wipe a sheen of sweat from his brow, and resolved to visit the baths later. For now, a snap of his fingers brought two men forward to stir the air around him with large wooden paddles. They followed him to the marble railing, where he again held out his hand. The air fleet officer standing behind him took a step forward and placed a pair of binoculars in his palm.

Resting the binoculars on the stone railing, he asked, "Kartinis, where should I be looking?"

Despite his youth, Air Fleet Captain Kartinis was both a veteran and a gifted advisor. Air Command had positioned him in the emperor's service to give them a strong, steady voice in the emperor's ear, and also to get him out of their hair. He was something of a maverick and had turned established Air Fleet doctrine on its head during several recent engagements. The emperor liked the young man because he reminded him of his younger son, Constantine. Who, Hadrian remembered, his smile darkening, had exchanged words with his father that they had later regretted. *Of course,* he sniffed, *he should be the one apologizing to me.*

Hadrian heard the clump of the officer's boots as he moved forward. "If Your Highness will look to the southeast," Kartinis said, pointing toward a large expanse of concrete just inside the city walls, "the *Marelena* is currently approaching the Aeroporto di Roma."

Hadrian swung the binoculars in the appropriate direction, where several bulbous shapes currently occupied the busiest air docking station in the Empire, possibly the busiest in the world. A smaller, sleeker airship was descending toward the field, its purple canvas balloon tapered at each end, its long gondola barely visible.

"The crew reported some problems with the boiler to steam conversion engine," Kartinis continued. The emperor appreciated the young officer's no-frills approach, and his solid, if occasionally unpopular or unlooked for, counsel. "It also reported that these problems had not been evident before takeoff. Your security chief did not think it prudent that we tempt fate by placing you on board." Several ground crew vehicles were now moving around on the concourse, as ropes dropped from the ship.

"I suppose there will always be anoth—"

A massive explosion lit up the field. The *Marelena* seemed to disintegrate in midair, the purple canvas blossoming into brilliant white-yellow light. Several seconds later, the pressure wave from the explosion reached the palace grounds.

"Get down, Majesty!" Kartinis pulled Hadrian to the ground. The explosion swept over them. Glass tinkled as windows in the palace were blown out.

Hadrian pushed Kartinis off of him while assuring the young man of his good health, and clambered to his feet. "Messenger!" he shouted. Several young men and women sprang forward. "You, get to the telegraph office. Find out what in Jupiter's name has happened. And tell the rest of the Empire that I'm alive. Now!" The man took off at breakneck speed. "You, you, and you. I want you to go down there and observe events firsthand. Report back to me personally. I want details. I also want to know whether this was an accident or a foiled assassination attempt."

"You could see if they need medical assistance," Kartinis suggested in a low but distinctly clear voice.

"That too!" the emperor added, eyebrows furrowed. "Learn everything you can. Then get yourself back here. *Move!*" The small group moved rapidly to comply.

Hadrian turned to the last man. "And you—I want you to go to the Legate Praetorius office and tell that meddlesome man that, one, he was right, and two, now he's got a massive problem to clean up."

As the man scurried off, he turned back to the air captain. "I want your immediate, unbiased opinion right this second, Captain. What happened?" Kartinis's Adam's apple bobbed as he gulped. He cleared his throat to gain time to phrase his response. Feeling his simmering anger rising to the boiling point, Hadrian demanded, "Air Captain Kartinis, what in Hades' name happened? Now!"

Kartinis took a deep breath. "Sire, as you have already stated, there are two possibilities. Either there was a major malfunction or it was a bomb or other explosive. Of the two, I personally believe it is more likely a contrived event. Although the crew did report having mechanical problems, the problems they mentioned would lead to a slow deflate, not an explosion of such immense proportions." Falling back on his training, he stood at attention.

Hadrian turned to frown at the air field. "Why explode it over the field? I was nowhere near the concourse."

"Majesty, we must look to your security. This place is too open. If indeed it was an assassination attempt, there may be a second attempt on your life. We need to move to the bunker, now." Kartinis was referring to the security bunker under the palace; any attacker would have to fight through hordes of security personnel and numerous defensive positions before gaining access to the emperor there.

Mention of an assassination attempt had sent murmurs through the Praetorian Guards in attendance, and Hadrian saw squads already encircling the Tower. Several more squads were arriving as Imperial guardsmen began setting up heavy repeating ballistae and training them out in all directions. Others moved to establish a shield wall around the Tower.

His face suddenly went pale. "What about my sons? Where is their security? They might be targets too!" Fighting panic, he began pacing erratically. *The security of the dynasty is threatened!*

Kartinis's steely, detached voice induced calm. "We still don't know it was an assassination attempt. We'll send a detachment to secure *Primus Caesar* Lucius and get him back here immediately. Other than that, we can send a message to Fort Tiberius, but *Secondus Caesar* Constantine is most likely safer there than we are here."

"Do it. And Kartinis, you lead it. Bring Lucius back to me."

Kartinis nodded, saluted, and turned. He strode away, giving instructions for several squads to meet him at the front gate as he left. Then, as if feeling Hadrian's urgency, Kartinis began to jog, then run toward the gate.

~ * * * ~

Primus Caesar Lucius lounged in the calfskin-upholstered viewing chair in his private viewing box halfway up the side of the great Roma coliseum. Here he enjoyed the cool fall breeze that pushed away the heat radiating off the metal bleachers full of plebeians and patricians stretching to either side of him. Fight day brought everyone out to watch the massive humanoid automatons battling in the center of the dirt-paved arena below.

Pistons hissing, brass, steel, and iron glinting in the sunlight, the mecha-gladiators circled, occasionally venting small spurts of steam. The crowd cheered or booed the fortunes of either the one bearing a red flag on its head, or the blue.

"I desire another drink, Aura; bring me one," he said to the scantily clad woman nestled next to him. Her full lips pouted as she slithered off him and moved behind him to tip the wine pitcher over his goblet. Condensation had formed on the glass from its cool contents. His two personal guards, standing at attention on either side of the box entrance, studiously avoided looking at her long, slender legs as she wiped her moist hands down her short skirt. *Let them look,* Lucius thought, already bored with his most recent companion. They never held his interest for more than a few weeks at a time, and this one was beginning to annoy him. Besides, if he kept her around too long, his father would press for Lucius to get married again. *Always worried about "securing the dynasty." Stupid old git.*

Lucius sat up in his seat as the blue mecha-gladiator swung a ten foot-long sword down at the other one. The red-flagged mecha-gladiator rolled to the left, then hooked its trident behind the leg of the blue one, bringing it down with a massive crash and screech of metal. The crowd roared approval as the trident-armed construct knocked aside the sword and crushed the shield of the blue automaton now lying helpless on the ground. Lucius could see the operator inside the grounded machine working desperately at his controls, trying to get his creation moving again—to no avail.

The crowd roared as the massive trident came down against the neck of the downed mecha-gladiator.

A monotone voice came from the speaker on the red 'bot. "Shall I remove him, Highness?"

Lucius held his hand out behind him and Aura placed his drink within his fleshy palm. He took a long sip while the crowd waited, anticipation building. He cleared his throat, then walked to the microphone. "Finish him."

The crowd's cheering surged as the trident lanced down, severing the head of the fallen mecha-gladiator. Steam shot into the air as the main control rods and boiler connection were severed. The body went limp, but the head rolled several times, finally coming to rest against the wall of the stadium. Several ground crewmembers rushed out to get the limp form of the defeated pilot out of his seat and hitch the parts of the now incapacitated construct to a steamtractor. As the tractor dragged the components from the arena floor, the triumphant mecha-gladiator marched around the arena, trident raised, striking poses to rile up the crowd.

I must get Father to let me buy one, or better yet, design and commission one, Lucius decided, riding the triumphant wave cresting around him.

BOOOOOOOOOOOOOooooooooooooooommmmmm.

A massive pressure wave washed over the coliseum on the heels of the deafening explosion, shocking the crowd and blowing dust, litter, and other debris into myriad dust devils. Many people fell; those who didn't raced for the exits, oblivious with panic.

"What was that?" Lucius blurted as soon as he'd recovered.

His guardsmen both shrugged. "Shall we return to the palace, My Lord? Or would you rather remain at the games?" asked Aestius, the more veteran of the two and in charge of his security detachment. His long black hair marked him as a man of Hunnic-Roman descent.

Lucius turned back to the field. The mecha-gladiator stood frozen in place. The stands were quickly emptying of people. Several bodies littered the aisleways, and sirens could be heard in the distance as emergency crews moved to deal with whatever had happened. "Let's get to the ostrichines. Whatever this calamitous event, it has undone the games. And I'm *bored*."

Aestius nodded and checked the entrance. The other legionary, Flavius, had unsheathed his sword and brought his shield around onto his left arm. With a curt nod from Aestius, Flavius took the lead as they stepped into the corridor behind the box.

"We'll meet up with the rest of the detachment, then get you out of here," Aestius said over his shoulder to Lucius as the heir moved to follow him, Aura on his heels. "That sounded like an explosion to me, and that can mean several things, none of them good for you or the city." Aestius' voice echoed in the narrow confines of the hallway.

When they finally exited into the main causeway, the rest of the guard detachment was no longer there. Aestius frowned. "Where are they?" Lucius asked. The guard would not have abandoned their posts for any reason. If pressed, they could have withdrawn into the narrow hallway and hidden or easily held off the mob inside the close quarters.

Flavius pointed to the ground with his sword. "Blood, sir. This doesn't look right."

Aestius went down on one knee and touched the blood droplets. His fingers came away smeared with red—the blood was still wet. He looked around, as did Lucius. Not another person was in sight.

"It's awfully quiet," Aura suddenly interjected, making Lucius and the other men start with surprise. "If we're going to leave, then let's leave," she complained.

Lucius looked to Aestius, whose jaw firmed as he made a decision. "This way, My Lord," he said, pointing along the causeway as he stepped forward himself. "Move quickly, now. I don't like the look of this. We have to get you out of here."

The more corpulent Lucius struggled to keep up with the fitter soldiers as they broke into a steady jog. Aura kicked off her shoes so she could move faster, and he struggled to keep up with *her*. Aestius led the small party down a staircase that brought them to the main concourse level. Lucius saw light ahead, and streets packed with people, raucous with noise and confusion. "This way to the ostrichines," Aestius called, leading the party around a last curve in the concourse.

Lucius paused to rest his arm against the wall. His lungs were on fire, and his breath came in gasps. "Come on, My Lord, we have to leave here, now!" Flavius pulled at Lucius's other arm, urging him forward.

They ran past overturned vendor stands below beautifully painted murals. Their feet clattered over tessellated floors commemorating the first mecha-gladiator battle. Then Aestius halted abruptly, throwing his arm up to stop the others. "Shhhhh!" he hissed, pushing Lucius and Aura against the wall. Flavius backed up and knelt down. "Listen."

Lucius heard voices farther down the concourse, close to the entrance. He leaned cautiously forward and saw a large group of armed men guarding the entrance. They were in legionnaire uniforms, but something didn't seem quite right about them. Flavius pointed to the weapons and whispered to Aestius about Gallic swords and small round bucklers that had gone out of style among even poor mercenary outfits long ago.

The two guards crept forward and listened for a moment, then pulled back. "They look like our guys, but they don't really act like them. They've got gear that isn't standard, and I don't recognize their accents," Flavius reported.

Aestius nodded agreement. "Could be Germans, maybe even Nortlanders, but I'm not certain."

"Nonsense!" Lucius interrupted. "Those men are legionaries and will be perfectly willing to help us get out of here."

"Sire, though we can't be certain, I'm pretty sure those are not our men. No moderately competent under-officer would ever allow his men to lounge about in that manner. And because we aren't certain, we can't possibly escape that way," Aestius insisted.

"Ridiculous. We shall leave by the front gate. I am the *primus imperio*. I demand that you follow my instructions."

He put every ounce of royal bearing into his voice. It wasn't much.

"No *sir*, my job is to protect you. I will gladly face your father afterward for insubordination if it means keeping you alive now. We're going to do the following ..." He laid out a quick plan, finishing with, "We'll escape through the lower entrance. They can't be guarding everywhere."

The party backed away from the corner and retreated to the last set of stairs. They descended. A short while later, Lucius found himself being guided through the facilities below the main level of the coliseum, still used by human gladiators who occasionally fought for pay—and died. The training yards were empty, but blacksmiths and artificers still worked down here, building, repairing, and modifying the mecha-gladiators that fought in the arena above them. It was darker here, the corridors more confined, those moving through them sounding like skittering denizens of the dark due to distance. They passed sputtering gas lanterns as they hurried toward the workers' entrance that opened at street level.

Several times, Lucius demanded a halt so he could catch his breath. Sweat had soaked his toga. "We're almost there, My Lord." Flavius said. "Once we're out into the city, we can conceal our identity, blend in, and get back to the Palace." Lucius nodded and reluctantly pushed away from the wall.

They entered a wider passage and Aestius pushed for a faster pace, their shoes clattering hollowly on the cobblestone floors and their shadows flickering ahead of them along the walls. They raced around a corner—the last corner before the exit, Flavius told Lucius—and stopped dead. A huge mecha-gladiator stood silhouetted in the maintenance entrance. Lucius saw the flag on its head and realized it was the same one that had been victorious in the earlier match. The massive trident was still held high in the air. A steel net hung in the other hand, ball bearings the size of a man's head weighting its edges.

No one moved.

"Sir, what should we do? Is it active?" Flavius asked Aestius. A dark stain of sweat made a V down the back of his tunic, and his spatha seemed heavy in his hand. After a moment he sheathed it and wiped his hands on his trousers.

Aestius looked around. Lucius followed his gaze, saw no other way out other than right past that giant, steam-powered death machine in front of them.

"We'll split up," Aestius said decisively. "I'll take His Highness right. Flavius, you take the woman left. We'll meet up back out on the plaza." Everyone nodded, and Aestius beckoned for Lucius to press his back against the left wall as Flavius and Aura crept to the right side.

"I'll go first, Your Highness. If for some reason I'm eliminated, keep moving. Don't stop. Run until you find somewhere you can hide. Someone will come rescue you. Do you understand me? You are more important than I. Do not stop for me."

Lucius nodded, his cold arrogance washed away by peril. This was life or death. It was not a play or a game in the coliseum. He would certainly not be coming back for any uncouth soldier, bodyguard or not.

Flavius looked over at Aestius. Aestius motioned him forward. "Go!"

The two pairs bolted toward the exit. They had just barely crossed into the sunshine when the mecha-gladiator moved. Pistons shrieking, it rotated, thrusting the giant trident at Flavius and Aura. Flavius raised his shield as Aura sprinted past him. The left tip of the trident grazed the shield, splintering it and hurling Flavius against the wall. He slumped there a moment, stunned, his left arm hanging limp. The trident stabbed into the wall above him, digging deep into the layers of brick and concrete. Flavius, still woozy, slithered out from under the trident and staggered forward. For a brief moment, the automaton's pilot tried to pull the huge weapon free, but its initial thrust had penetrated the solid Roman construction so completely that it was a lost cause.

Lucius and Aestius sprinted past, then continued running across the marble-paved plaza. Aura caught up with them. Lucius, wiping brown hair now slick with sweat off his forehead, took a quick look behind him. Flavius, still shaky, was approaching—but so was the mechanical gladiator; it had turned and was taking great strides toward them. It would catch Flavius any second now.

"Keep moving!" Aestius shouted.

Scrambling across the road, they ran toward the massive complex on Palatine Hill. "Get out of the way!" roared Lucius as a steam hauler stopped just short of them. If they could just get to the Temple of Venus, they could hide amongst its towering columns. Fixing his gaze on the two large Venus mecha-statues on either side of the temple's large, ornate doors, Lucius moved toward them with the others, then hesitated as a scream split the air behind them.

The mecha-gladiator had caught up to Flavius, who had turned and swung his sword in a useless gesture of defiance. The pilot brought the automaton's free hand around and swatted Flavius aside as if he were a bug. The young man flew through the air and crashed into the side of the steam hauler. The impact left a dent in the side of the vehicle. Its operator bailed, bolting across the pavement and out of sight. Flavius slid to the ground and lay in a crumpled heap, blood leaking from his helmet.

Aestius cried out when he saw Flavius fly through the air. Pedestrians fled in all directions. With adrenaline pumping through his veins, Lucius found new strength, and led the remainder of the party onward, away from the death machine.

A shadow fell over them.

Lucius turned his head to see the massive net dropping down around them, just before its weight knocked them all to the ground and engulfed them, knocking Aura unconscious. He struggled to get to his feet, but the heavy net weighed him down and cut into his skin. Scrabbling for his belt knife with sweat-slick hands, Lucius finally freed it and started slicing at the net's thick metal strands. Aestius soon joined him, hacking away with his long curved cavalry sword. *We only need to free one strand,* Lucius thought desperately. *Then maybe I can squeeze through and escape!* He looked at the tight weave of the net. *Okay, two strands, then I can escape.*

Screech, screech, screech. Sparks flew as the two men worked hard to cut the metal cables. Lucius's arm burned with the effort. Beside him, Aura moaned as she slowly regained consciousness. The twined wires gave way just as a shadow loomed up behind them. Aestius glanced upward, then pushed Lucius through the gap. Then he turned to face the monstrosity.

Without pause, the mecha-gladiator reached down—and squelched the veteran officer. Shards of wood and metal shot like projectiles into Lucius' exposed legs as the guard's shield shattered. He screamed in pain, then scrambled away on all fours. Her dress soaked with the dead bodyguard's blood, Aura crawled out of the gap behind him. The automaton's pilot raised the mecha-gladiator's arm, gears and crankshafts whirring as it moved closer. Lucius crawled faster.

Aura suddenly gave a high-pitched laugh. Lucius turned his head to see what was happening. The mecha-gladiator had stopped and now seemed to be waiting for something.

"Quick, Aura! Help me up, we've got to get out of here," Lucius ordered, his voice raw with panic and pain. He gasped when he saw the bloody gashes crisscrossing the backs of his legs.

Aura moved closer, carrying Aestius's discarded spatha. "I'd be glad to help, *My Lord*, but I'm just your paid wench, someone to be used and discarded. Isn't that what you were thinking earlier? Hmmm? I'll show you how I feel about being discarded." With that, she plunged the spatha into Lucius' chest.

The blade bit deep. Searing pain sucked the ability to speak, to make any kind of sound, away from Lucius for a moment. But only for a moment. When she yanked the sword out, he screamed. He stared down in disbelief at the red stain blossoming across his white toga as blood gushed from the wound. "Why ... how could ...you ..." He choked, gurgled, drooled blood. Its bitter tang filled his mouth.

Aura stabbed down again. Lucius felt everything go hazy. His eyes rolled back and he stopped thrashing.

~ * * * ~

Aura dropped the sword. She stepped back, chest heaving as she sucked in great ragged breaths. She stared a moment at the two dead bodies, then turned to the side and was noisily sick. A few moments later, she wiped her mouth and looked up at the hulking mecha-gladiator. A large brass arm came down and settled gently on the ground next to her. She nodded up at the pilot's chair.

A mechanical voice said through a speaker, "This is but another great moment in the cause of liberty."

Aura nodded, looking down at the corpse of the heir to the throne. She felt a brief moment of sadness that was quickly replaced by joy. She had succeeded where others had failed. "Shall we make our getaway?" she said lightly.

In response, the cockpit opened and a middle-aged man stepped out. He climbed down the hand, using the many armored segments like a ladder. They came together for a quick hug, then they raced off, disappearing into the crowd now pressing closer to the scene of the assassination.

~ * * * ~

Captain Kartinis and his crew arrived five minutes too late. Looking up at the mecha-gladiator standing quiescent next to the bodies, he knew that, even had they shown up in time, their weaponry would have been insufficient against the monstrous automaton.

Around them, people in the crowd wept openly; others simply stared, grim-faced. Leaving half of his command to contain the scene and recover the heir's remains, he began the slow ride back to the palace. He spent the journey trying to figure out how to break such tragic news to the most powerful man in the Empire.

Alas, there was no easy way.

CHAPTER

9

THE SPEAKING TUBE GURGLED. The officer of the day leaned forward in the command chair and unstoppered the device to listen. The voice was teeny but clear as it exited the tube: "Sir, I have a skimmer on the horizon. Colors are friendly. It's flashing the pass code of the week."

First Officer Travins confirmed and restoppered the speaking tube. He turned. "Captain, topside lookouts report a skimmer coming this way. Recommend we come to a heading west-southwest for the landing."

"Very well, Mister Travins, follow the landing procedures. Have the stern batteries manned as well and extend the landing platform." Captain Alexandros opened the bridge portal and moved toward the landing dock at the stern of the ship.

Claxons began to wail. Red lights pulsed, splashing the hallway with the color of blood as men donned vests of light flak armor and raced to their battle stations. A squad of airmen raced past, their apologies lost in the howl of a ship coming to combat readiness. By the time the skimmer had circled the airship *Scioparto*, the retractable landing platform had been winched down from the open rear decks and extended out. Two large steel arms held the narrow wooden platform firmly in place.

The skimmer pilot brought his small recon vessel directly under the aft portion of the dirigible. Two rotating propellers on either side of the main body kept the small skimmer stable as it gently descended onto the landing platform. The whine of the engines cut off, and the propeller blades slowed, then stopped. The mechanical arms holding the platform began retracting. Finally, with a bang of steel and wood meeting, the landing platform returned to its original place. A squad of airmen trained to act as ground crew moved forward, securing the skimmer to the deck with thick ropes run through loops on the deck. "All secure!" shouted the senior enlisted man on deck.

Alexandros studied the skimmer, which looked like a cigar that had grown wings and spouted large barrels on either side. The end of the skimmer was wasp-like and needle sharp. It was possible, technically, for a skimmer to kill an airship by "stinging" it to death. With the exception of the "stinger," engines, and glass cockpit window, the skimmer was created entirely from wood to save on weight. To further save on weight, the craft were piloted by boys and some girls between the ages of twelve and fifteen. Although established Air Fleet doctrine, Alexandros thought this was pure idiocy. Who in their right mind expected a thirteen-year-old to understand the military complexities of a battle? Their brains had not yet developed enough to function fully!

Realizing he was philosophizing again, Alexandros quickly brought himself back to reality and watched two crewmen help a small figure from the cockpit.

The pilot strode toward Captain Alexandros and stopped before him. The young man's head barely came up to the medals on the older man's uniform. "Sir, request permission to board your airship, *Captain!*" The last word came as a squeak as the boy's voice cracked. His hand came up in a crisp salute that stopped just short of the bill of the wool and leather flying cap on his head. Several nearby crewmen sniggered as his voice broke, and the lad's face colored, but he did not give in to the temptation to chew out the technically junior deckhands.

Alexandros returned his salute. "Permission given. What is the nature of your visit? You have a private message?" Alexandros doubted that; most messages could be exchanged through the wireless set just off the bridge—although it had been quiet for the last few hours.

"Sir, the message is to be delivered only upon my decision that the location is secure and private. Is there someplace we can talk?" the boy asked. This time his voice didn't squeak. He rubbed his hands together and looked around, the gesture making him look older, until he added plaintively, "Perhaps somewhere out of the wind?" Skimmers were not exceptionally warm at any altitude, or in any season.

Smiling, Alexandros gave a crewman an order to go to the galley and round up some food. If he remembered anything about his teenage nephews, it was that they were always hungry. While his crew stood down from their battle stations, the captain strode back into the shelter of the bridge, the young pilot on his heels. The portal closed behind them, cutting short the wind gusting across the platform. The pilot sighed.

"Recon Pilot Second Class Fero Juvas Garius, sir," the boy answered when Alexandros asked him his name. "Based at Fort Tiberius on the skim launcher *Praecedo* under Wing Commander Silenia Juna Octavia."

Alexandros nodded. He had met the wing commander, briefly, at a soirée held in Roma a few years back. She was incredibly young, but she had an exceptionally strong sense of strategy and was ahead of the curve of many of her classmates at the Northern Fleet Command's Air Academy. She was also an incredibly gifted dancer. He smiled at that memory.

They climbed up a level to Deck B, stepping off the ladder to walk down the short hallway to the captain's quarters occupying the stern quarter. An armed airman posted at the door saluted and swung the door open with an accompanying, "Sir."

Alexandros nodded at him. "We're expecting someone from the galley in a bit. Please knock and send them in, Airman Yanis."

As the door slid closed behind them, he walked behind his desk and took a seat in the leather chair. He leaned back. "Now, what message do you have?"

The young man shuffled through his messenger bag and pulled out a metal cylinder, sealed at both ends. One end had a keyhole. "If you'll excuse me, sir, I'm not allowed to know the contents of the message. I'll step out for a moment. If you need me, I'll be in the hallway." Pilot Garius saluted again, turned on his heel, and left the room, closing the door behind him.

Alexandros stared at the secure message capsule. He reached under his uniform and pulled out the Captain's Key dangling on a thin golden chain. Northern Command's keys were shaped like snowflakes. Rotating the snowflake until a key slid from one of the snowflake's prongs, he inserted it into the lock and turned it. A satisfying *click* sounded and the container cracked open. He opened it fully, extracted its contents, and set the tube itself on his mahogany desk. He turned on the electric light next to him, leaned back in his chair, and began to read.

MESSAGE PRIORITY: URGENT

TOP SECRET CLEARANCE REQUIRED – FOR EYES ONLY

MESSAGE ORIGINATION: ROMA – FLEET COMMAND – MEDDITERANEAN HQ

MESSAGE RECEIVED: BRITTENBURG – NORTH CENTRAL OPERATIONS HQ

RETRANSMIT TO FORT TIBERIUS – XIII GERMANIA LEGION HQ

MESSAGE SENT VIA COURIER TO RECIPIENT

TO: CAPTAIN ALEXANDROS, H.M.A.S. SCIOPARTO

ASSASSINATION ATTEMPT ON EMPEROR, 23 OF SEPTEMBER

STOP

SUCCESSFUL ASSASSINATION OF PRIMUS CAESAR LUCIUS

STOP

SECURE SECONDUS CAESAR IMMEDIATELY UPON RECIEPT OF MESSAGE

STOP

RETRIEVE SECONDUS CAESAR CONSTANTINE IMMEDIATELY FOR RETURN TO ROME

STOP

USE ANY AND ALL METHODS TO SECURE SAFETY OF SECONDUS

STOP

POSSIBLE INFILTRATION OF SECURITY PROTOCOLS

STOP

DO NOT INFORM OTHERS OF SECURITY PENETRATION

STOP

MAY THE GODS' SPEED BLESS YOU

STOP

SIGNED – AIR FLEET ADMIRAL IGNAEUS, AIR FLEET HIGH COMMAND

COMMUNICATIONS WATCH OFFICER – TRANSMITTER BRUTUS SILENIUS, XIII GERMANIA LEGION

ORIGIN AND TRANSMISSION RECIEPT SHOULD BE DESTROYED IMMEDIATELY AFTER ACKNOWLEDGEMENT OF ORDERS

TRANSMISSION LOGGED 13:45:12 ON 25 SEPTEMBER, 1856

END TRANSMISSION

After reading it for the tenth time, Alexandros finally lowered the paper with a trembling hand. *Oh ... my ... gods.*

An attempt on the emperor's life, and the *primus caesar* was killed? That meant that the *secondus caesar,* who happened to be one of Alexandros' new friends, was the next man in line for the Laurel Crown.

He pulled the plug out of the speaking tube protruding through his desktop. "Officer on duty," he called.

"Janus here, sir," came the instant response.

"Do we know where the 13th Cohort is training? We need to pick them up, immediately. Uh ... urgent orders from HQ. And see if you can raise the cohort on the wireless. Let them know to be expecting us." He wasn't an exceptionally good liar, and in general preferred to be open and honest with his men, believing that it was good for morale and built a tighter crew. This case was a tad different, however.

"Right away, Captain," Second Airman Janus responded.

Alexandros replugged the speaking tube. Then he reached down and slid out the drawer next to his left leg. He pulled out a glass bottle and a tumbler. Setting the tumbler on his desk, he unstoppered the bottle and poured a small dose of fine, aged whiskey into the tumbler, then tipped it down his throat. He poured himself another and drank it more slowly as he regarded the missive from HQ. The background hum of the engines suddenly rose as they increased speed. Alexandros felt the ship adjusting course to a new heading.

A knock on the door prompted him to carefully fold the message into a small square and tuck it into his breast pocket as he called, "Enter."

Airman Yanis entered bearing a plate of food. He set the food down on the desk in front of the captain and exited the room. Alexandros stared at his food, suddenly lacking any appetite. He replaced the whiskey and the tumbler in the desk drawer, then closed the message container, locked it, and slipped the snowflake key back under his uniform. He lifted the plate of food.

He stepped out into the corridor, where Pilot Garius sat on a stool with a plate of food on his lap. "Yanis," he said to the airman beside him, "let the boy eat until he is full. He can have mine as well. Don't let him leave yet, though. When we reach our destination, I'll have a return message for him."

Yanis nodded as he accepted the captain's plate. Ignoring the young pilot peering gleefully at this second helping, Alexandros set course for the bridge.

~ * * * ~

So this is what it feels like to be on guard duty for twelve hours straight, Julius thought, his brain muzzy from lack of sleep. The cohort had been taking part in the required "extended wilderness survival" training, during which a cohort was left alone in a remote location for a limited time to practice how to establish a base camp and become self-sufficient. Tribune Appius had been placing some squads on extended guard duty rosters to free up others for hunting and reconnaissance.

Julius paused in his patrol route and leaned on his plumbata, gazing at the rolling hills and copses of trees that surrounded "Fort Altus," named after the reconnoitering soldier who had sat down in the middle of the vast farmlands of Germania Inferior and declared, "We're building here because I'm not walking anymore." Julius's eyes drooped and his nodding head settled against the iron head of the plumbata. *I'll just put my head down for a moment ...*

"Hey, Caesar! Don't be falling asleep now! Less than an hour to go, my lad." Legionnaire Horace called out to him from the tower.

Julius started, shook his head, and resumed his walk toward the corner tower.

"Why don't ye come on up and take a look at the view from my marvelous wooden throne?" Horace joked.

Julius sighed. Horace was one of the new recruits who had been added to their unit halfway through training. Several days ago, word had come down from the general that he wanted the 13th to be an over-strength cohort, especially since it would be unsupported by the rest of the legion in its rapid assault role. So, sure enough, the other cohorts in the legion had taken advantage of the order by sending the most troublesome, argumentative, and lazy legionnaires they had. Horace was a castoff from 17th Cohort.

Julius looked up at him. "Sure, why not?" He climbed the lashed-together ladder that provided access to the tower and accepted Horace's friendly hand at the top.

Horace patted a gauntleted hand on one of the iron walls that enclosed the wooden frame of the tower. "The walls are just high enough to making sitting *and* leaning on them uncomfortable. You think they designed them that way?"

Julius shrugged. He walked over to the telescope set up on a tripod in the middle of the platform. Each tower had a telescope, a modification suggested by Centurion Vibius. Tribune Appius had quickly agreed to the foresight, and now the tower guards were able to see for miles in any direction, regardless of eye strength.

The two men chatted, careful to remain several feet apart and face in different directions so that any roving squad leader or centurion wouldn't find fault with Julius's new post. *Of course, Horace would be blamed as well, since misery loves company in this man's army,* Julius thought wryly as he stared out at the horizon. It really was beautiful.

Horace said something that brought his attention back from the landscape. "Sorry, say that again?"

"Geez, Caesar, got wool in your ears? No, wait, you're a factory cog, so I suppose that would be grease in your ears." Horace laughed. "I asked, what made you join the army, and how did you end up in this here 'experimental' unit?"

He was an original member of the cohort, Julius told him; he had joined the army out of a sense of duty, patriotism, and, he added with some embarrassment, because he was bored.

"And you aren't bored now?" Horace teased.

Julius sensed an insult and countered with, "What about you? You got transferred in. Must have pissed somebody in the 17th off big-time. What did you do, sleep with the centurion's wife?" *So there!* Julius thought. *That ought to shut him up.*

Horace's smile revealed several missing teeth among the yellow survivors. "Actually, it was the sister, but I won't make your virgin ears bleed with such tales of debauchery."

Julius snickered and shook his head in amazement. What some men did for fun was insanity to him.

"You ladies having a picnic up here?" a steely voice called up from the ladder. A moment later the centurion's head appeared above the platform.

"Sir!" Both men stood at attention and saluted. Centurion Vibius frowned at them. Julius sucked in a breath, waiting for the dressing-down he knew Vibius was about to launch.

Beside him, a wide-eyed Horace threw up his arm. "Sir! Begging your pardon, but there's an airship on approach." He pointed to the southeast.

Vibius turned to follow his outstretched arm with his eyes. Julius squinted, releasing the pent breath in a slight gasp. In the distance, sun glanced off a tiny black speck that had appeared from behind a clump of foliage. Horace carried the tripod over to the tower's east side and adjusted the articulating legs, then stepped back. Vibius leaned over the eyepiece and rotated the interior lenses using the small dial on the side of the brass tube. Julius could imagine what Vibius was seeing: the distant airship leaping into view, perhaps sending a critical message. Or was this part of the exercise?

Vibius pulled a pad of paper and a grease pencil out of his pocket. "Do either of you two know how to write?" he asked. Julius nodded hesitantly. Vibius handed him the pad and pencil. "Copy down exactly what I tell you to."

Julius handed his plumbata and shield to Horace, who adjusted his own arms to accommodate them without comment. "Ready, sir."

"N ... c ... y ... p ... i ... c ... k ... u ... p ... a ... l ... e ... r ... t."

Julius wrote all the letters down, but only a few things were popping out for him. Centurion Vibius continued deciphering more letters.

"E ... m ... e ... r ... g ... e ... n ... c ... y—okay, they are starting to repeat now. Did you figure out the message?" Vibius asked.

Horace was peering over Julius's shoulder. "Caesar here has written gobbledly-gook," he exclaimed. "I don't know what ncypick means."

Julius shoved him with his shoulder, knocking the man off balance. "That's not the word. It says 'emergency pickup alert.' What does that mean, sir?"

Vibius seemed to tense. Julius could see lines of concentration forming at the corners of his eyes. The centurion moved over to the pneumatic siren mounted on the tower parapet and began to rotate its lever. With each rotation, the siren gradually increased in volume, starting at a low whine and growing to an ear-splitting scream. It instantly dashed Julius's sleepiness. Below, the camp burst into a bustle of activity. Men ran this way and that, snapping on armor and lacing up boots.

Vibius stopped the siren and ordered Horace, "Get down there and inform the tribune that we have company. Recommend we prepare to close up camp." Horace nodded and slid down the ladder, feet not even touching the rungs.

"Stay up here, keep an eye on them, and sing out if they change course for any reason," the centurion said to Julius, who nodded and moved to occupy Vibius's position as the centurion followed Horace down the ladder, shouting commands as he went.

Julius ducked his head to look through the viewfinder at the airship as it inched closer. *What are you doing here? What has happened?* he wondered.

~ * * * ~

The airship took the extraordinary step of actually landing in the meadow next to the small hill where the 13th had constructed their base. They moved the entire cohort into the ship, filling the airship to the brim with men and equipment, both on the outside decks and inside, clogging the hallways, storage rooms, and crew quarters. Two hours later they were ready to depart, leaving behind a muddy, rutted hilltop littered with the occasional piece of discarded or forgotten equipment where a small, standard pattern legion fort had stood.

Word had circulated through the 13th very quickly that something had happened. The airship crew professed innocence and rebuffed any further attempts to learn more. The legionnaires were of two minds. One opinion was that the crew legitimately knew nothing. The second opinion was that the crewmen knew and were ordered directly not to tell anyone. Most men around Julius seemed to believe the first as the more likely, since most airmen were about as tight-lipped as an opera singer.

Julius was packed into one of the forward weapons bays, tight against the metal hull of the airship. Third, fourth, and fifth squads were packed into the bay like sardines. Julius wondered if the ship had come for the entire cohort, or just the tribune. Tribune Appius had been spirited away with the airship captain almost as soon as the lines had secured the ship to the makeshift landing zone.

A legionnaire sitting nearby pulled out a pack of cards. "So, comrades, who is ready to lose some money?"

~ * * * ~

One deck above, in Captain Alexandros' quarters, Tribune Appius absently swirled fine Hiberian whiskey in a tumbler. "You're certain this message is genuine?" he asked for the fifth time.

"Completely, Your Lordship. It came on the proper letterhead and the security procedures were followed. They even used a skimmer to get it here. That's a top-level message, as genuine as you can make it. So I have to believe it's the truth." Alexandros paused and took a sip of his whiskey.

At a buzz from the plugged speaking tube, he leaned over and uncorked the tube, listened for a second, then acknowledged the message with a curt, "Go for launch." He looked at Constantine. "We're ready for liftoff. Everyone is on board."

The tribune nodded, then took another sip of the fine liquor. It burned down his throat, but helped ease the pain of discovering he was now the last surviving male heir to the Appian Imperial Dynasty. Utter sadness crept up on him.

He had never really gotten along with his brother. They had been born several years apart, and enjoyed different interests. The older Lucius had been groomed as the heir to the throne since he could walk. Knowing the fate of a nation rested in his hands tended to change a person's outlook. *Of course, in his case, that fate rested in his large and meaty hands,* Constantine thought. *I suppose this means I'll have to leave the legion. For the first time in my life, I finally felt like I belonged somewhere.* Another part of Constantine countered, *You have a duty to your father and to your nation. Do not whine and complain because of the circumstances.*

Captain Alexandros had been watching him. Now, in an obvious effort to bring the tribune out of his somber musings, he said briskly, "Come to the bridge with me to watch the takeoff. You'll get a great view."

Constantine nodded and silently followed the captain as he slid open the oak-paneled door and walked down the hallway, squeezing past crewmembers and legionnaires alike, airmen saluting the captain and the legionnaires placing fist to chest for the tribune. This ship was a beehive of activity, and it took the better part of ten minutes to get from the captain's quarters aft to the bridge in the forward compartment.

"Captain on the bridge!" cried a petty officer near the hatch as they entered.

"At ease, resume your duties," Alexandros said quickly. "Are we ready for liftoff?"

"Ready and awaitin' your orders, Cap'n," the watch officer informed him. "Ballast tanks are full and all compartments are secured. Helium Division reports all is ready and chambers are at full capacity. We're as ready as we can be."

Alexandros nodded. "Excellent, Mr. Flanos. Take us up, please; one-half thrust."

The officer opened the speaking tube to the engine room and relayed the captain's command. Constantine felt the vibration in the flooring as the steam boiler's crankshaft was connected and the massive propellers began to slowly rotate at the rear of the ship.

"Ailerons to full raised position. Anchor lines off. Close helium bleed-offs."

At the control panel, engineers rapidly moved levers to different positions, each one connecting with a clank. Toward the rear of the ship, behind the massive propellers that were generating more and more thrust, several rudder components moved, forcing the air from the propeller toward the ground. The ship rose. With the helium no longer being vented, the ship hovered just off the ground, gaining a few inches each second.

"Buoyancy is positive; we are gaining altitude," called a watch officer. "Dumping 10% ballast."

"Steady as she goes; this is an easy climb." The captain calmly paced along the deck to stand near one of the large observation windows.

Constantine felt the vibration in the deck beneath him grow to a low rumble. His body shifted balance as the ship tilted fractionally upward, and he reached out to grasp a convenient handhold hanging from the ceiling. The tilt of the deck increased, though none of the airmen appeared bothered by the incline. *They must be so used to it.*

"Altitude at fifty feet. Sixty feet. Still rising."

"Level off at seven hundred feet. We'll swing south and proceed to Fort Tiberius. Any report of bad weather?" Alexandros asked from the window, his hands clasped behind his dark leather flying jacket.

The watch officer opened another speaking tube bearing a small copper plate labeled *Topside Lookouts*. He shouted into the tube, then pressed his ear against the opening, trying to hear the answer over the constant hum of the engine and, Constantine presumed, the wind outside. The officer replaced the tube cap and looked up. "Topside lookout reports partial cloudy skies but no gray or black ones in sight, sir."

Alexandros nodded. "Let's get a move on, shall we? It's not like we've got all day!" He chuckled.

The *Scioparto* ponderously turned its bulk to a southeastern heading. With the ship now on its appointed course, the hustle and bustle on the bridge calmed somewhat.

Constantine let out a breath he hadn't realized he had been holding. It was nothing unusual to him to ride in a dirigible, but the weight of the entire situation was finally settling fully over him, leaving him feeling drained. He looked through the observation window on a world that seemed to be going gray before him. "I think I'd like to sit down for awhile," he managed to mumble.

~ * * * ~

Alexandros turned from the window in time to see the tribune crumple slowly toward the floor. "Quick, someone catch the man, he's got altitude sickness!" Alexandros barked, hoping to distract his crew from conjecture. Two men leapt to comply, grabbing the tribune's elbows and keeping him from hitting the deck.

"Let's just sit him right here," Alexandros said breezily. "Pass the word for the doctor to come have a look at him, but otherwise it will probably be best if we simply let him rest for the remainder of our flight." *I hope no one wonders why he never had altitude sickness before this point,* Alexandros thought, careful to keep a frown from his face. *Regardless of how he's feeling, it's my job to get him back to Fort Tiberius in one piece, his secret intact.* "And pass word for Centurion Vibius, as well," he continued. "He'll want to take his commanding officer back to my cabin; young man looks like he could use a spot of sleep, eh?"

When the tribune had withdrawn, arm slung over the centurion's supporting shoulder, Captain Alexandros paced the forward observation windows, for a moment enjoying the marvelous view of the Germania Inferior countryside. *This is what the gods see when they look down at us.* He imagined them staring down at him from an even higher vantage point, and took a moment to say a brief prayer. Although he did not consider himself an exceptionally pious man, he had a special affinity for the goddess Minerva. *Thank you, Minerva, goddess of wisdom, for granting me this chance to remove the stain upon my family's honor. It is a pleasure to serve you, and the cause of justness, in your name. Please help us with our journey, and watch over the young prince, for he needs our guidance and wisdom more than ever.*

At that moment a tailwind sprang up, propelling the *Scioparto* even more rapidly toward Fort Tiberius. Almost as if, Alexandros noted, the goddess had answered his prayer.

CHAPTER

10

C LINK.
The tiny sound of drinking glasses touching in a toast broke the silence of the warehouse. Several members drank to Deus Ex Mortalitas. As one, they put down their small tumblers.

"Operation Teutonburg is in motion. We are strong, and we are ready. Let us show those imperial fools just who is in charge," Brimmas Amalia told her followers. "I want a status report on all our operations, right now. We must be ready to move by this evening." She paused. "By now, some of you may have heard that our operation in Rome met partial success."

The words prompted a burst of chatter, with several members looking at each other, some with shock, others with glee.

"S'cuse me, but what do you mean by partially successful?" asked the weedy-looking scribe, Klavius. "What went wrong?"

"Our operatives had a problem getting to the emperor. They were unable to eliminate him. However, they did succeed in wrecking the main areoporta in Rome. They will be unable to move units out of the city by air for several months."

"And what about the primus caesar?" another rebel asked.

Amalia smiled, cold and smug. "He has been taken care of, in the best possible way." Her laugh echoed around the cavernous warehouse, making the rebels loading ammunition into some stolen walkers pause. "Although only partially successful, we have actually created a new opportunity to eliminate the other heir." He voice dripped with scorn. "Because daddy dear is so worried about him, he has ordered the young Constantine back to Rome for his protection. We know this because our agent intercepted the message." Again she paused, noting the querying looks on some faces. "This plays right into our hands. We have the last surviving son of the emperor walking right into the city that is about to be ours." She smiled.

"Corbus, the map, please," she called. Corbus unrolled a map onto a nearby table. The council gathered around, staring intently at the intricate, hand-drawn floorplans.

"Chief Jaix Extraci, you will lead the gangers against the palace. Remember to wait until you hear the explosions before storming the gate. If you succeed, kill everyone inside and loot the palace—anything you find is yours to keep. If you cannot do it immediately, wait until our walkers can come up to crush the gate."

She turned to the industrialists. "Domino Hunostus, I trust you have drivers for our walkers ready to go?"

"Yes, Domina Amalia, we have the walkers modified and crewed, as per your directions. Your son," he gestured toward Corbus, now leaning against a steel column, "has seen fit to provide me with some of his best recruits. We'll be ready, and until then, they'll be discreet."

Amalia nodded thoughtfully. "Get them moving now. We have received the confirmation from our Nortland allies—they will be here within the next few hours."

The gangers and Hunostus left to see to their operations.

"Excuse me for asking, but how can we prevent the Imperialists from calling for backup?" another industrialist asked. "How can we stop the legions from arriving to save the day? We cannot take them in a one-on-one battle, regardless of our ingenuity and determination. As I said when I agreed to fund this venture, I want my guaranteed return on investment. In money, not in blood." The rings on his fingers sparkled as he wrung his hands together for effect.

"The same source that gave us the information about the arrival of Secondus Caesar Constantine also happens to be on duty today at Fort Tiberius. Not only can he read any messages, he can also choose what to send and when to receive any other messages. Should any loyalists get out an alert, he is well placed to prevent the nearest Imperial forces from responding. Not that a green legion with no veterans would truly be able to launch an effective rescue. Everything is well in hand, Lunis; you will get your money." Her tone ended further complaints.

She stared down at the paper. In the blink of an eye, she had drawn her knife and stabbed it into the middle of the Brittenburg governor's mansion. Smiling coldly, she looked around at their faces and said in a voice as frigid and sharp as ice, "So tell me, my friends: who is ready to deliver the next of many death blows to the largest empire on earth?"

~ * * * ~

Not too far away, Tribune Appius was suffering death by a thousand cuts. He was enduring a small soiree at the governor's mansion. Although he would have preferred to wait at the airport, Constantine had been invited to join the legate governor and several of his closest political flunkies and friends. Industrialists in top hats and trim black suits mixed with toga-clad city and provincial officials. Several women in attendance had tried to catch Constantine's eye, but he found none of them the least bit attractive, even when dolled up with the latest makeup and poufy ball gowns. He had always preferred the more traditional, simpler dresses devoid of folds of lace.

If one more sniveling person tries to tell me why I should invest in his new thingamajig or whatchamacallit ... Constantine's hand clenched and red wine slopped over his fingers as the thin, decorative silver goblet fractured. "Pah!" he mumbled to himself.

A moment later his aide was next to him, holding a small towel. "Here you go, sir, let me get you a fresh cup of the red," the legionnaire whispered.

"No need, Manus; I've gone and wasted this one." He handed over the damaged goblet, glancing furtively around at the modest gathering of people in the main audience chamber. Several ladies giggled as they sauntered past, eyeing the two soldiers up and down. One was even wearing those new tall-heeled shoe contraptions, swaying unsteadily like a tree in a gale.

"Is there anything going on out there," he jerked his head toward the outer door, "that could get me out of this pointless frivolity? I've had it up to here with these people."

Manus gave a small smile. He looked thoughtful for a few moments, then moved in close, eyes also darting around. "Well, sir, I daresay that you could ... er ... inspect the perimeter and central defenses in place here against a possible attack? Safety first—and I hear there are bandits about," he added with a cynical grin.

For the first time in quite a while, Constantine smiled. He looked up from his hands, the towel ruined with red wine stains. "I suppose for the safety of all involved, most particularly my sanity, that I shall be required to observe all current safety procedures being undertaken here at the governor's residence." He turned to face the crowd, taking a steadying breath while Manus stepped back a few paces.

Ding, ding, ding. He tapped the hilt of his belt dagger against the ruined goblet to attract the crowd's attention. A hush descended over the room. Constantine waited a moment before speaking. "Ladies and gentlemen, it appears that I have been remiss in my duties as both an officer and a fellow Roman. My aide has informed me that I have not yet performed my required perimeter inspection of the villa and grounds. As the ranking military officer present, it is mandatory that I complete this duty, for the safety of all, and of course, for the comfort of all here." His voice rang out, but inside he was quivering, knowing his excuse was weak and flimsy.

But polite applause rewarded him. Shouts of "Absolutely!" and "Good thinking!" followed him as he moved toward a side exit. Women gushed about how brave and heroic he was. *Seriously? I'm taking a walk and all of a sudden I'm heroic?*

The legate governor appeared before him as he passed between several fluted columns. "Good afternoon, Legate Vorcentus," Constantine said in a neutral voice.

The portly legate acknowledged with a nod. "Tribune. I see duty waits for no one. It is a shame to see you leaving so soon." His voice was a low rumble. He pushed some graying hair out of his eyes. "Of course you'll be returning to us shortly, I suppose?"

Constantine nodded regally, though he grimaced inwardly.

"I remember when I was in the legions, how we never had a moment's repose," the man began. "Have I told you about the time I led the IX Hispania against the remnants of the Azorean raiders? Talk about a battle! Why, we were outnumbered three to one, and I ordered ..."

Once, the legate governor had been a model soldier, outstanding general, and strong ally to Constantine's father. Now he was a slightly addled, unfocused, and only moderately competent governor. Constantine nodded at appropriate points in the legate governor's rambling, feigning interest. *At least it's better than dancing.* Though he'd excelled at fencing, Constantine had never been able to comprehend the exotic and terrifying grace required for dancing. His father, who had firmly believed his youngest should know how to act like a gentleman, often commented upon his missteps and intricately impressive failures at dance.

Eventually, he spied Manus, caught his attention, and flashed him a pointed look. Manus immediately complied.

"Excuse me, sir," the aide interrupted in his most annoying, officious voice as he joined Constantine and the legate, "but you really must be getting a move on. You know how important it is that you fulfill all of your required duties."

Constantine inclined his head to the legate, who appeared startled at being sidetracked. "Duty calls."

They left the stuffy and crowded ballroom. "This way, sir. I'll take you to Auxilia Centurion Quintus. We can see the whole city from the operations center. It's a great way to pass the time." Legionnaire Manus led the way to a small complex in the middle of the gardens composed of a tall observation tower surrounded by an eight-foot wall and a barracks facility.

The complex was not extensively fortified, but secure enough for the fifty-member demi-cohort assigned to guard the legate governor. They entered through its only gate and stepped into a small courtyard, where Auxilia Centurion Quintus met them. Legionnaire Manus explained the situation.

"Not a problem. I'd love to give you a tour of our facilities here. I know they can't hold a candle to the Imperial Palace in Rome, but then again, I don't have four thousand crack Praetorian Guardsmen at my command." He offered a wry smile as he took them up the observation tower.

"I can see the entire perimeter from here, and we've got several patrols out right now," Centurion Quintus continued as they reached the top. "Obviously, we work closely with the constabulary to monitor any dissident groups or more organized gangs." He gave them a brief overview of the security procedures and various points of interest as they moved around the tower, the wooden and steel frame creaking slightly beneath their weight.

"Uh, sir," called Manus, "you might want to take a look at this."

Quintus and Constantine moved over to west side of the tower.

"Did we have any airships scheduled to move in today? And if so, why are they shelling the city?" Manus asked.

Quintus looked confused, while Constantine fumbled for his binoculars. He slammed them up to his eyes so quickly, he winced in pain as he trained them on the two large cargo dirigibles. Bolts lanced out from the gondolas at mid-ship, striking random targets below. He could feel the slight vibration running up the tower from the ground as the sounds of the explosions reached their ears.

Quintus ran to the speaking tube and unstoppered it. "We're under attack!" he shouted into it. "Scramble all divisions! Contact the constabulary and reserves immediately! Do it, now!" he screamed when a voice at the other end apparently questioned his orders.

He rejoined Constantine, who proffered the binoculars. Accepting them gratefully, Quintus trained them on the western part of the city. "They almost look like Nortland raiders, with those weapons," he mused after a moment. "We're too far away to tell, though."

The sound of hooves clattering along the cobblestone path drew their attention downward. A soldier leapt from the horse and disappeared from view below the tower. Seconds later, a squawk from the speaking tube grabbed their attention. Quintus picked up the receiver. "What? When? Get two squads over there right now!"

From the courtyard below, Constantine heard the jingle and clang and thud of men strapping on armor and assembling into their squads. An alarm began to wail.

"There is a mob at the main gate. They tried to get in earlier, but the guards managed to shut the gates. What in Pluto's name is going on?" muttered Quintus.

Manus held out his hand for the binoculars and aimed them at the gate. "Sir! They're throwing rocks and debris; it's flying over the wall!" The mob was beginning to stretch its muscles.

"Where did they all come from?" Quintus asked, shaking his head in bewilderment.

Constantine frowned, his mind racing. Airships, convenient mobs, the death of my brother ... He voiced his thoughts. "I don't think those two events are unrelated. I think someone's plot just came to fruition. We're going to have to think fast. Quintus, do you have a wireless connection? We'll radio the XIII Germania for assistance. They are the nearest force that we can trust. I'd bet the constabulary has been infiltrated. We can't rely on them fully." He fired the words from his mouth as rapidly as he thought them, his brain in full crisis mode.

Quintus gulped, then spouted a new set of orders into the speaking tube.

"Manus, I want you to—" A larger explosion grabbed Constantine's attention. He grabbed his binoculars and pushed them back up to his eyes.

Something large and mechanical was moving toward the mansion. "Quintus, any chance you happen to have some ... heavy weaponry in your arsenal?" he asked.

Quintus turned, looking confused until Constantine handed over the binoculars. "What is that thing?" Quintus sputtered, lowering the binoculars. The middle-aged officer was beginning to look overwhelmed. "I suppose we've got some heavy-duty ballistae kits in the armory," he told Constantine. "We'll have to check. They are probably disassembled, so we'll need time to set them up."

Constantine nodded. "Let's get moving, then."

The three men raced down the spiral staircase, taking the steps two, sometimes three at a time.

"This way to the wireless room!" Quintus called as they ran into the main operations building. He paused to detail two men to go back up to the observation tower to maintain a lookout. Two squads, now fully kitted out, passed them as they marched double-quick toward the main gate. They rounded a corner and sidled into the tiny wireless room, where two men sat twisting dials and tapping away at various buttons.

The senior member turned to them. "Sir, we've been unable to raise the XIII Germania. Something appears to be wrong with their gear. We know they are receiving the alert messages, but they aren't confirming or responding or anything. What else would you like us to do?"

Quintus looked at Constantine, his shoulders slumped.

"Could we try to get to the airfield and get you out in a skimmer, sir? Your safety is paramount," Manus suggested.

Constantine shook his head. "Remember those columns of smoke we saw? I'm fairly certain one of them came from the airfield. It is a logical first target for any attack or revolt. The rail link is down too, due to that sabotage the other week."

The mood in the room was gloomy. Then Constantine brightened. "Legionnaire, do you have access to the Air Fleet frequencies?" he asked.

Both wireless operators nodded hesitantly. "We aren't supposed to, but I have a few friends in the service with whom I traded codes, one time," the younger man admitted.

Constantine smiled. "I think I've got an idea ..."

~ * * * ~

The wireless set in the message room of H.M.A.S. Scioparto squealed. The dozing operator nearly fell out of his chair as a message came over the airwaves. He scrambled for a grease pencil and scribbled down everything he could get. His eyes widened in shock as the message continued. Finally the machine fell silent. The operator took a moment to wipe his hand across his now sweaty forehead, leaving a line of grease from the pencil under his airman's cap. Almost automatically, he activated the wireless and sent the "Message received and acknowledged" indicator.

The young airman read the message in its entirety again. Then he reached over and pressed the red-alert button on the wall. Klaxons began to wail throughout the ship. Steeling himself, he opened the speaking tube from the bridge. "Sir, I've got something I think you should take a look at."

~ * * * ~

"We've received a confirmation from the Scioparto. Looks like we may be getting assistance after all, Centurion, sir," the operator confirmed, looking back up at the officers.

"Very well." For the first time, Centurion Quintus seemed calm. "We've got a battle to win." He turned to march out, but paused to order the operators to send out the Request Assistance message on all frequencies until either they were dead, or lost power. "At the very least, we'll jam their responders so full of our message that they won't be able to communicate!" Quintus boasted. "We'll blast that out over the airwaves."

The small command team left the wireless room and exited the small barracks. The remaining men of the governor's guard met them in the courtyard.

An under-officer saluted Centurion Quintus. "All present and accounted for, sir. Where do you want us?"

Quintus hesitated, glancing at Constantine. "Your Lordship, as the highest ranking officer present, I hereby pass command of the garrison to you. What are your orders?" he asked.

Constantine nodded his acceptance, then considered their options. "I assume the only entrance in or out is the main gate? Or is that too much to hope for?"

"There is a small servants' entrance on the eastern wall. It's lightly guarded, but the gate is strong."

Constantine's brows furrowed. "We better get a squad over there, just in case. Manus, go with them. Sing out if you hear or see anything." Manus nodded, his face glinting with a sheen of sweat. "I want you in temporary command as well. Don't leave your position, don't open the gate, and don't do anything stupid. Understand?"

The young legionnaire straightened his back and saluted. "Sir, yes, sir!"

A squad under-officer saluted him and they marched off through the gate, leaving the courtyard almost empty. Just a few men of the guard cohort awaited their orders.

Quintus pulled Constantine aside. "Sir, there are a few others here who would be willing to contribute to the defense. It's a bit unorthodox, but ..."

Constantine raised an eyebrow. "Do you mean that you would arm civilians to help us out?"

Quintus nodded. "Absolutely, sir. It looks like we'll need every man we can get, untrained or not. Besides, sir, they've armed civilians." Seeing the logic in this, Constantine agreed.

Quintus stepped away, and projected his voice into the courtyard. "Alright, boys, time to get to work. I want the arsenal open and emptied. Get all the heavy repeaters and as many explosive-tipped plumbatae as we can carry. Buldrix, Vespansis, get over to the servants' quarters. I want every man who looks capable dragged back here and equipped. It's past time to be picky about service. Tribune Appius here has assumed command of the entire garrison. I'm going to go to the mansion and round up any volunteers or ex-military men." He dropped his voice and winked at Constantine. "I know a few favors I can all in, if need be."

He turned back to the remainder of the guard cohort. "Don't wait for me, get those reinforcements to the wall." He leapt onto his ostrichine and galloped away, the machine's metal feet digging into the perfectly manicured lawn.

Constantine waited ten minutes for Buldrix and Vespansis to get back. Several messengers from the front gate had been back and forth, speaking of a situation getting ever so desperate. The noise and smoke coming from that area supported their assertion that the garrison was being hard-pressed by the rioters.

Finally, the two legionaries returned, herding about twenty older men and boys before them. They really are scraping the bottom of the barrel now, aren't they? Constantine thought. He ordered them equipped, and quickly returned to the wireless room.

"Any news?" he inquired.

The wireless operators looked frazzled. "We're sending messages out constantly, sir, but no one is responding. Not even the Scioparto. We could be jammed and not even know it."

Constantine nodded. "Well, that's a risk we'll just have to take. Get yourselves equipped. If the main gate falls we're coming here, and you'll have to be ready to fight."

One operator's face went as white as a bed linen; the other's hands started to shake. "We ... we have to fight, sir?"

Constantine grimaced. Are these men soldiers, or just boys in soldier's clothing? "Not what you signed up for?" he snapped. "Last time I checked, you were both soldiers. Now get out there and act like it." He turned and marched back to the courtyard, both operators scrambling after him.

"Attention!" Constantine's voice rang from the gray stucco walls. Men around the yard came to attention, several dropping boxes and weapons in their haste to obey. "Form ranks, prepare to march," he ordered.

About thirty men assembled in a haphazard fashion. Constantine was instantly able to pick out the actual legionary members from their drafted counterparts. He sighed. They would have to do. They look like my men did only a few weeks ago, he reminded himself.

Leaving behind the wireless operators and a skeleton crew made up of the doctor and Infirmary cases, Constantine moved his ramshackle demi-cohort toward the front gate.

Gray smoke rose ominously over the tall perimeter walls. A fitful breeze brought the smell of burnt wood and metallic char from burning buildings. Gritting his teeth, Constantine pushed his men harder, trying to ignore the draftees who lost their equipment as they struggled to keep up. Finally, panting from the effort, the straggling group reached the front gate.

The governor's mansion had not been built as a fortress. Its wall was simple and narrow, meant to ensure privacy and prevent trespass. There was no room to stand upon it, no parapet. Two towers flanked the largely ornamental front gate. They were twice as high as the wall, or about fifteen feet high. Several soldiers stood atop each, huddled behind shields as they fired crossbows into the crowd storming the gate, which was barely holding together. The defenders had scrambled to reinforce it with anything available; Constantine identified the bronze heads and stone pedestals of priceless garden statuary wedged amidst a tipped produce cart and several bodies.

Spying the approaching reinforcements from his position at the gate, a harried-looking under-officer called to Constantine, relief etched on his face, "Thank the gods you've arrived. Where are the rest of you? We can't hold out much longer!" Beside him, soldiers strained to keep the gate shut, shoulders to their shields, pushing back against the unseen crowd shouting its displeasure on the other side.

"I'm Tribune Constantine Tiberius Appius, ranking officer and dinner guest," he said as he joined the under-officer. "We're all that's to be had. Where do you need us the most?"

The officer's shoulders sagged. "You're all that we've got?" he asked hoarsely. "Where is the auxilia, the constabulary?"

Constantine looked around at the ragged remnants of the gate guard and the previous reinforcements. He knew something was needed. "Probably out there somewhere. In the meantime, we'll take as many of them with us as we can. That's all the emperor expects of you." He jerked his chin toward the gate. "Those men are beyond the emperor's pardon now."

Exhausted men came down from the towers as fresh new men took their place. The under-officer, a sub-centurion named Halix, gladly surrendered command to Constantine, and brought him up to speed.

The rioters had appeared early that morning, but at first they were peaceful, simply a large crowd milling around. They had not hassled those leaving or entering the grounds, even when the rich and mighty had gathered to honor the now Primus Caesar Constantine. "And then, when those two cargo airships started bombing the city," Halix pointed at the cargo airship visible from their location, now busy eliminating city garrison positions along the wall, "the crowd suddenly got violent, and—well, you see where we are now. They just tried to use a battering ram, but they've pulled back for a moment." He pointed to the smoke and haze slowly building over the rioters. "They're lighting trash and rubble fires."

"Sir! You need to come and see this!" a legionnaire shouted from one of the towers.

What could it be now? Constantine asked himself. Things can't get any worse, can they? He climbed the ladder up to the crowded platform. His hands slipped on blood as he tried to find purchase on a bloody rung. A strong hand reached down and Constantine accepted it gratefully.

"Not a problem, sir," the legionary said as he hauled the tribune up onto the platform. The iron tang of blood and the stale scent of fear assaulted Constantine's nostrils, driving out the smell of smoke and belying the legionary's comment. "But you'll want to take a look at this."

Constantine fiddled with his binocular case. "See the smoke and fog over there?" the legionary said when he'd finally extracted the optical tool. "We saw something moving in it earlier, but now it's coming closer."

Across Brittenburg's large central plaza, the mob was gathering again. Constantine lifted the binoculars to his eyes. In the smoke, he could just make out several large, segmented legs and a brick-like body. Central Waste Collection was painted on its side. Was that the mechanical monstrosity he had seen earlier? "Why would they have a garbage collection vehicle here? Are they planning to burn it?" he wondered aloud. He swept his binoculars along the distant rioters.

"Get down, Tribune, sir!" several men shouted at once. A hand grabbed his cloak and yanked him back and down; he landed on the platform, his arms and legs splaying every which way. A long shape flickered overhead and disappeared behind them.

Constantine brushed himself off and knelt next to the parapet. An explosion shook the tower. "Where did that come from?" he asked. Another soldier pointed to the trash hauler. Constantine sighed. He worked his way over to the side facing the mansion grounds. A fresh crater was still smoking in the lawn, about fifty yards behind the gate. He turned back to the front line. Things had just gone from bad to worse. "Who on terra turns a trash hauler into a war machine?"

CHAPTER

11

THE FATES WILL BE BUSY today," Captain Alexandros said. Acting Tribune Vibius, temporarily commanding the 13th Rapid Assault and Response Cohort of the XIII Germania Legion, nodded in agreement. "The men are ready, you just have to get us into position, as close as you possibly can," he said. "Remember, my men are still essentially unblooded. A scrap with another cohort does not make them into a veteran unit."

Alexandros turned to the acting tribune. "No need to worry, Vibius; this is not my first ball. I'll make sure your lads get into battle with nary a scratch nor a blemish on 'em. But we have to get them there first, and that involves my full attention. Now, if you will see to your men, I will see to my ship."

Vibius saluted and removed himself from the bridge, boots clomping on the metal deck. Alexandros turned. "Bring us up to combat speed," he ordered. "I want us to take out at least one of those fat cargo flyers before they have a chance to double-team us."

He reached down and pulled a lever. "All hands, we are now at battle stations. Chiefs, inform your divisions and arm all weaponry. Aim for the gas bag—let's try to take her down in one swoop." *Gods, please don't let those fat bugs be double hulled. We might not survive that encounter.*

The *Scioparto* had been running at full speed ever since she had received the distress call from Brittenburg. Alexandros had thought quickly, dispatching several messengers to the command center in case the saboteurs had friends. In fact, upon receiving the report, Legate General Minnicus himself had questioned the wireless operator who had failed to pass on the increasingly desperate messages from the city. The man was soon turned over to the intelligence division for further interrogation after inconsistencies developed in his story—such as wireless equipment that worked perfectly, once he was removed.

The general had instantly realized that they needed a way to reinforce the city fast. His decision to put the 125 untested men of the 13th Cohort at the vanguard was both controversial and risky, but it was the only chance he had of getting any soldiers to the city in time to be helpful. So while the rest of the legion formed up to be loaded onto a requisitioned express steamtrain, the 13th boarded the *Scioparto* in full combat rig, prepared to drop into an urban war zone, the most dangerous type imaginable. Which had already had Captain Alexandros sweating.

Now, he gripped the armrests of his captain's chair and stared down at the airship looming ahead of them. Moments after coming within engagement range, he had already revised his opinion of the capabilities of the usually sluggish cargo flyers. His suspicion that they were, in fact, Nortland Karlock-class raiders was confirmed the second he saw the first bombs dropped from the large, boxish gondola amidships. *They look like the newer class, so they are probably double hulled. We're going to have to take them out the old-fashioned way.*

"Get us nice and close. I want to eliminate his ability to respond before he realizes he's lost it," he told the helmsman. The veteran airman gripped the copper and wooden helm tightly, moving the *Scioparto* slowly, slowly closer, directly from behind.

136

"Move to his port side; I want us screened from their friend closer to the bay," Alexandros ordered. The bridge fell silent as the crewmembers around him gazed out the observation windows with anticipation, like him, no doubt praying that their opponents were too busy wreaking havoc on the undefended city below to notice the smaller *Scioparto* sliding up next to them. With no defensive fire from the city ramparts whose defense towers burned like torches around a ring, Alexandros heard the hum of the engines, the shuffle of crewmembers passing out in the hallway, and little else.

"We're in optimal firing range, sir," the weapons officer on the starboard side reported.

This close, Alexandros could see the painted designs and cleverly disguised artillery ports. Several were open, but the launchers were aimed downward; occasionally, explosive-tipped bolts flew down onto the buildings below.

"Captain, markings indicate she is the airship *Thorolf.* Definitely a warship," the watch officer called.

"Very well, she is a combatant, then. All starboard batteries, fire at will!" Alexandros ordered.

The weapons officer twisted a dial and a green light flashed along the starboard weapons galleries. "Fire!" cried the artillery deck officers. Repeater scorpion launchers and heavier, single-shot ballistae threw everything they had at the unsuspecting Nortlander vessel. The repeater launchers aimed for the gasbag and glass-enclosed bridge, their five foot-long, steel-tipped darts shattering the glass to pierce those crewing the raider and destroy equipment. Glass shards flew everywhere, incapacitating many of the deck officers and killing others. Another artillery crew got a lucky shot right into the weapons gallery facing them, destroying weaponry and severing several steam conduits.

Alexandros's well-trained crew maintained an intense volume of fire, rapidly emptying boxes of ammunition that were quickly replenished from the centralized arsenal. Each package of bolts contained ten shots, which a crew could use inside of two minutes. Occasionally, a scorpion threw a bolt or required a spring replacement—such heavy use in a short period of time strained them immensely.

Complementing the faster-firing scorpion launchers were the explosive throwing ballistae. The gun crews took more care and time here, as a dropped shell could mean an explosion inside their own ship. The loader winched down the U-shaped holder and nestled the black powder-filled iron egg into place. The gunner then carefully selected his target, allowing for gravity and wind, found the trigger with both hands, and fired.

One of these iron balls careened across the space between the two ships and hit right next to a crew compartment. The impact shook the enemy ship as the explosion tore a jagged hole between two decks.

A few launchers returned fire from the beleaguered Nortland ship. It was sporadic, but it kept the crew of the *Scioparto* on their toes. "Brace for upshot!" Alexandros shouted, and the warning to the airmen below to find a handhold was relayed, even as the ship abruptly lifted upward as the *Scioparto* dumped ballast, gaining about a hundred feet on its floundering opponent. Alexandros smiled. The artillery crews on both decks could now hit the exposed topside of the raider. The crews again went to work, quickly eliminating the small topside ballistae positions and shredding the thick canvas of the gasbag.

The ship was in major trouble now, and the artillery fire from *Scioparto* paused as the ship below them rapidly lost altitude. Even with a double hull, the gasbag was punctured in too many places for the airship to stay aloft. The dying ship descended toward the central plaza, eventually crashing through apartment complexes and sliding along a major thoroughfare, spilling men, steel, iron, and other airship components everywhere. Parts of the ship crashed through a mob of people in front of the gates of the governor's mansion.

The crew's cheers filtered into the bridge as the officers congratulated Captain Alexandros.

"Excellent work, sir. You really pulled a fast one on them!"

"They never saw it coming!"

Alexandros allowed a tight-lipped smile as their enthusiasm bubbled over. Then, "Simmer down now, gentlemen; we've only won half the battle," he reminded them, and they returned to their seats.

"Sir, bottom-side lookouts report the mob is trying to enter the governor's mansion," an officer reported. "It appears to be held by guardsmen, but they are having a rough time of it. If we shift course to heading seven two point four eight, we can support them with our lower deck weaponry."

Alexandros thought for a moment. "Let's be even more bold. Bring us about right over that main structure down there. It's open enough for us to drop the 13th, and we can support the loyalist forces. Pass the word for the 13th to drop, full combat rig. Topside lookouts are to keep an eye on that second ship. I don't want it to even look our way without us knowing about it."

Men jumped to their jobs. The bulk of the ship turned and assumed position over the mansion.

~ * * * ~

A messenger moved through the crowded hallways, the cargo holds and crew rooms, looking for Centurion Vibius. The men he passed were silent, struggling to deal with nerves and stress. Most could only shake their head when he queried the centurion's whereabouts.

"He gathered his squad leaders and took them to his bunkroom to plan the combat drop," one of the legionnaires finally told him.

When the messenger found the room where the centurion was supposed to be, he stopped, aghast. The compartment had been hit by one of the last desperate shots from the *Thorolf.* The cabin was a chaos of blood and shattered glass. Two crewmen were quickly hammering plywood sheets over a large hole where half the outer wall had been. Six figures lay on the deck. Someone had found small laurel branches to place on the bodies. A medico from the ship's Infirmary was quickly checking the lone survivor standing on the far side of the room.

"I'm looking for the centurion," the messenger said hesitantly.

The single remaining legionnaire looked up at him, his face streaked with smoke and blood. "I'm the highest ranking officer left. Acting Centurion Julius Caesar."

"He's alive only by luck," the medico added curtly, not stopping his examination to look at the messenger. "When the explosive projectile hit, he was behind several bunk beds, getting a drink of water. It saved his life."

And in that moment, the acting squad leader was promoted to acting centurion, the messenger realized; not a move for the faint of heart.

The messenger recoiled as the young man turned and puked into a bucket. A moment later he straightened, wiping his mouth with the back of his hand. The messenger looked away, his eyes falling on the bodies. A medical corpsman was now covering the last one with a tarp, shaking his head. The sight of the dead man's charred clothing combined with the smell of burnt flesh made him queasy, and he nearly needed the bucket as well.

Desperate to get out of there, he turned back to the legionary and asked, anxiety making his voice sound impatient, "So are you the commanding officer, or not?"

Julius squared his shoulders and picked up his fallen helmet. He placed it firmly on his head and buckled the strap. "Yes, I'm acting centurion. What are our orders?"

"Captain Alexandros offers his compliments, sir, and begs leave to inform you that your men are to be ready to drop in five minutes." He paused to check his timepiece. "That order was given three minutes ago, sir. The ship cannot remain on station for too long, as there is still another enemy airship out there."

Julius's mouth sagged open.

"Can you do it?" the messenger asked, the question almost a squeak.

Looking down at his dead comrades, Julius murmured, "There's no one else to lead. We'll be ready."

~ * * * ~

After the messenger left, Julius listened to the hammering of the crewmen patching the hole, too numb to move.

As he walked by, the medico paused to put a hand on Julius's shoulder for a moment and say a quiet prayer. "I'll send someone to collect the bodies," he said, dropping his hand. Julius thanked him, and the medico left the room.

Julius wasn't ready to leave yet. Kneeling, he pulled back the shroud covering Vibius and tenderly detached the brass centurion pin. He said a silent prayer of his own, then rose and attached the pin to his shoulder as he strode from the room.

Grabbing the first legionnaire he saw, he mustered his strongest command voice. "Assemble the men on the jump decks. It's past time we leave this flying tub."

He looked around. Word had spread rapidly about the deaths. The loss of most of their officers was a hard pill to swallow, and several men looked mutinous. Julius knew how they felt; *he'd* be unwilling to drop into a war zone without the right leadership. Now, though, he had no choice. He thought for a second, then raised his voice. "You know, the tribune is down there, waiting for us to hurry up and save his high and mighty behind. Let's get a move on, people!" He punctuated the last word by slamming his gauntleted fist into his open palm.

The men began grabbing gear and moving toward the drop lines. The crewmembers were already out there, and wires descended from the ship like spider silk. As Julius stepped out onto the top deck, a midshipman reported to the bridge that they were ready. The recently promoted Julius was now left with figuring out what to do on the ground.

He began marshaling the men into line. "Adueinus, make a space over there! Dapelicus, check those men's gear—one of them appears to have his carpteneo on backwards. We can't have that. Gwendyrn! Get your lazy backside over to this line. You'll be leading it down!"

Julius leaned in close as Gwendyrn scurried forward. "I need someone I can trust on the ground. Standard deployment, secure the area. If it looks clear, take half the first team and secure that gate," he ordered in a low voice. Then he said louder, "I'm giving you a battlefield commission to 1st Junior Centurion, 13th Cohort. I need a competent man to be my second. No going crazy now, you hear?"

Nearby men chuckled, but it did little to erase the tension in the air. Julius felt like a fraud. Public speaking was not his thing. He strained to sound like the tribune had during their first airdrop, back in training. "You are the assault team. This is a historic moment; we are the first rapid response unit to ever drop into combat. Are you going to insult our forefathers? Shame your parents? Disgrace your families?"

A resounding "No!" came back to him.

"Good! Junior Centurion Gwendyrn will lead the first team. Follow his orders as if they came from ..." Julius knew he did not carry much sway with his men yet, so he improvised " ... like they came from our Tribune Appius himself! He is down there, fighting his way through hordes of traitors and foreigners. They have given up any right to be called Romans. I say we go get him, and show him what real Romans can do!"

Cheering, the men of the 13th Cohort attached themselves to the drop lines. Airmen held tight to the railings as they fought to keep the lines from swaying in the wind.

A green light illuminated on deck. It cast an eerie green glow over the assembled men. "Go! Go! Go!" shouted the airmen, and the men attached their carpteneos to the lines and leapt off. Looking like beads on a thread, they slid down toward the open gardens of the mansion.

Centurion Caesar borrowed a pair of binoculars from an airman and swept them along the wall toward the gate, where the mob had recovered from the impact of the *Thorolf* and again pressed forward, using a battering ram against the barrier. No doubt seeing the arrival of their allies, small

*You are the assault team. This is a historic moment; we are the
first rapid response unit to ever drop into combat.*

figures ran to and fro, redoubling their efforts to hold off the mob, although the defensive fire had slackened in the last few minutes.

"Hurry up, Gwendyrn, get those men in position," Julius muttered. The bottom deck of the gondola blocked his view so he couldn't see the men right below the ship, but he knew they were all grounded by now. He swung the binoculars back to the gate and watched anxiously as the rioters succeeded in cracking an opening between the two panels. The defenders were thrown back from the gate; enemies trickled through the opening, leaping over several injured men sprawled in the dust.

Hold them! he cried silently. *Just a bit longer!* A pitiful handful of men rushed to the gate, repeater crossbows laying down a hail of fire. For a brief moment or two, the press at the gates slowed as rioters went down, arrows slicing through linen tunics and canvas overalls. The wounded screamed in pain as they were trampled beneath the crowd surging forward. Their ammunition out, the defenders dropped their crossbows and charged, spathae and shields against bricks and clubs.

A tap on his shoulder made Julius whirl away from the drama unfolding at the palace gates. A senior enlisted airman stood waiting, holding a carpteneo. "Sir, the first batch is down," the airman told him. "We can't stay on station much longer. The crosswinds are beginning to affect our ability to remain stationary."

Now that his attention had returned to the airship, Julius did notice that the engines were louder, working harder than before. He nodded, then quickly pulled the goggles down over his eyes and buckled his chinstrap. The airman patted his equipment down, making sure there was nothing loose or unsecured. With a return nod, the airman led him over to the drop point and handed over the carpteneo, saying, "Don't forget your slider, sir."

Julius allowed a small chuckle. The things had been in use for less than a month, and already they had a new nickname. He turned back to look at the second wave of legionaries, all geared up and awaiting his orders. "What are you waiting for, an invitation?" he quipped as he reached out and clapped his carpteneo onto the thick cable. Drawing a deep breath, he stepped out into space.

Without the support of the deck, he could feel the same crosswinds buffeting him that were beginning to pummel the *Scioparto,* the second he cleared the ship. He looked up at the ship, rapidly dwindling above him, the coppery tint of the glasses casting it and the rest of the world in sepia tones. He made out the damage the dirigible had suffered in its battle, then turned to survey his hometown. What he saw made him cry out in anguish.

Brittenburg was burning. Debris from the fallen Nortland airship had created a trail of devastation that served as the spark. Flames glowed in stone alleyways, moved along awnings, and licked through elaborately decorated mansions. A warehouse went up in a fiery ball of gas and vapor, the flames blue against the dark smoke covering the city.

Julius checked his height on his wrist altimeter. He was approaching the red zone, or stop zone, where you were supposed to slow your descent to a reasonable speed. A tight squeeze on his *slider* (he liked that term better), and he felt his momentum slow. A few final spurts deposited him roughly on the ground.

A legionnaire was there to meet him. "Sir, Junior Centurion Gwendyrn's compliments. He begs leave to tell you—and this is a direct quote sir, so please excuse the language—'If you are done lollygagging, get your slothful soldiers here, or we'll have done all the work for you.'" The soldier stopped and looked sheepishly at Julius, anticipating an angry outburst.

Instead Julius gave a grim smile. "He never learns. We only sent him ahead so he could get some much needed practice. We'll be along as soon as possible. Tell him that I want his men ready to push out against the mob. If we push them hard, we'll break them, I think."

He thought that would be the best idea. Theoretically, if he could push them out of the narrow confines of the gate, he could bring the greater skills and training of the Roman legionnaires to bear on the dangerous, but untrained, rioters.

As a new recruit, Julius had been given only rudimentary tactical training with his peers, as it was assumed officers with advanced training would be available to lead and give orders. Unless a new man proved exceptionally gifted, it was rare that further training would be provided. Julius had not been one of those exceptionally gifted men; he'd just been considered above average when it came time to choose squad leaders.

Gathering his men, he ordered repeater crossbows unslung and loaded. The men quickly assembled their weapons.

Julius felt a twinge of pride. In less than ten minutes, an entire Roman cohort had performed an airdrop into a combat zone, and prepared for battle. In a more peaceful time, there would have been an extravagant ceremony with a day off for the men. Now, a single comment would suffice. "That was good, but next time I want it under eight minutes."

They were close to the gate, so they quick-marched closer, their iron-toed boots pounding over the cobblestone pathways and thudding across grass lawns. They assembled behind the thin line of steel-armored legionaries holding the entrance. The crowd had backed off somewhat at the appearance of this new threat, allowing the ragtag group of palace defenders to pull back to rest under a makeshift tent while the 13th Cohort took their places and their medics saw to the injured.

A man in a dress uniform stood and walked over to Julius, pulling off his oversized helmet as he got close. Julius recognized that brown hair and the even more familiar nose. "Sir?" Julius choked out, forgetting to salute.

"Good to see you too, Legionnaire Caesar ," Tribune Appius replied. "But where is Centurion Vibius? Forgive me for asking, but did the cleaners mix up your uniforms?"

Julius was then forced to relive his moment of shock and pain in the crew cabin— the explosion, the blood, the desperate attempts to save lives—for the tribune's sake.

Tribune Appius sadly shook his head. "They were good men. We will mourn them and pay our respects to them later. The least they would want now is for us to do our duty. Every son of Brittenburg must now be willing to defend it to the utmost." His voice seemed to ring from the guard towers. Then he dropped it to a more intimate level to add, "Especially you, our newest centurion."

He must have learned that trick from his father, Julius thought. *The emperor is a great orator. Does he feel phony when he does that?* He realized the tribune was waiting for him to say something, and fumbled for words before he managed to say, "Sir, I turn the cohort over to you." He executed an awkward salute that involved shifting his crossbow from one hand to the other.

The tribune saluted stiffly, then quickly got down to business. "I want every man available up on those towers. Does anyone have a speaking trumpet?" His query raised eyebrows. Several men were dispatched to locate a speaking trumpet and a few minutes later a legionary handed one to Constantine that he'd dug out of the tower storeroom.

"Sir, what are you doing?" Julius asked, alarmed, as Constantine checked to see if it worked. *I'm now the one responsible for the life of the heir to the Roman Empire. How on earth did I end up with that job!?*

"Why Julius, my lad, I'm going to go demonstrate the triumph of reason over anger and violence," Constantine stated in a haughty voice.

Julius didn't try to keep the doubt from showing on his face. "Really, sir?" His voice was dead monotone.

Constantine lifted his eyebrows at him. "No need to take that tone with me, *Centurion*," he said as a subtle reminder of who was in charge, although Julius thought he saw a sparkle of humor in those ice-gray eyes.

Julius watched the tribune climb up the western tower. A piercing *squuuuueeeeeeaaaaaaaaalllllllllllll* indicated that he had turned on the trumpet's speaker. Men instinctively slapped their hands over their ears, even though most were wearing helmets. Several glared up at the tribune.

Oblivious to the distress he had just caused his own men, Constantine turned the speaker toward the crowd. "Now hear this. All people in the plaza are to disperse and return home immediately. Brittenburg is under martial law, and anyone caught out on the streets will be subject to deadly force." The trumpet made his words sound hollow and distorted.

Murmurs rose from the crowd. Several on the periphery tried to slip away, but men in gang paraphernalia grabbed them and pushed them back into line. Several of the ruffians waved weapons or anti-Imperial banners.

Constantine tried again. "If you return home now, no one will be punished."

Someone in the crowd shouted back at him. That voice was joined by several others, as the more vocal protestors hurled insults back at the Imperial officer. Vegetables and fruits flew threw the air, then cobblestones and bricks.

Gwendyrn ducked behind his shield. He turned back to face Julius, disgust puckering his face. "At least they haven't tried to storm the gate again. What's left of it, that is," he remarked wryly to Julius.

A clattering sound drew Julius's attention back to the tower in time to see the tribune hastening down the metal ladder. He waited for Constantine to join them before asking nonchalantly, "So, Tribune, sir, how did reason fare over violence and anger?"

The tribune grimaced. "We'll just have to reinforce the lesson with a bit of old-fashioned corporal punishment." A thousand-throat scream of fury and belligerence interrupted him.

He ran back to grab the discarded speaking trumpet. This time he addressed the defenders. "Ready, boys—remember your training! Keep your thrusts short and cover your brothers. Repeaters, I want as much fire as you can place on those rebels. Aim for the leaders if you can!"

The guttural screams rose in pitch. "Here they come!"

CHAPTER

12

THE NEW DAY DAWNED MUDDY with gloom over Brittenburg. The pall of smoke from the burning buildings and factories lay heavily upon the once glittering jewel of the Roman Empire.

Centurion Julius Brutus Caesar shook off the fatigue that threatened to engulf him. He was one of a line of tired men who stood facing the square. The rioters had thrown themselves against the cohort again and again. Just when the Imperials thought they had the upper hand, a new threat appeared. A small force of Nortland raiders and well-armed and equipped rebels had stormed the posterior gate, and succeeded in breaching it.

The messenger from legionnaire Manus had barely managed to get away, but he'd informed the rest of the cohort in time; they'd met this new danger head-on in the gardens, and a nighttime running battle ensued. The 13th Cohort had lost its formation and been battered by the individualistic Nortland savages, but numbers finally began to tell—the lines had stabilized and the legionnaires had cut down the attackers. The battle had ended just now.

Julius had remained at the main gate with barely twenty men, feigning a strength that was not there until the remainder of the mob had slowly dispersed. There were scarcely a hundred die-hards on the other side of the plaza, looting stores but not bothering the entrenched cohort.

An injured soldier moved up to the Julius's position. They had continued to use everyone, except the most critically injured, to fill gaps in the line. Julius could see the bloodstained bandages peeping out from under helmets and wrapped around hands and arms. Thanks to their superior training and heavier armor, the legionnaires had suffered fewer injuries, although almost everyone was battered black and blue under their heavily dented armor.

"Message for the tribune. I can't locate him, so I found you instead, sir," the man said, his voice unapologetic and hoarse. He adjusted the sling on his right arm with a tug.

"Thanks, Tramais. Hold up one minute." Julius opened the folded sheet of paper with grimy hands, careful not to smudge the words. He pushed his helmet back off his head so he could see the small lines of printed text, and read slowly, wishing he were a faster reader. *I'm going to have to borrow books from someone. I can't look slow in front of the other officers now,* he thought, suddenly conscious that he had not received the best education. Even the legions needed men who could read and write, as well as swing a sword.

By the time he had finished reading, legionnaire Tramais had settled on a broken piece of statuary. He pushed to his feet when Julius turned to him. "Take this to the tribune immediately. Please tell him I'll be gathering what people I can spare at the fountain," Julius said, referring to the large fountain located in the middle of the palace grounds, making it a convenient assembly point.

"Sir." Tramais saluted awkwardly with his left hand and left to find Tribune Appius.

Although he was a slow reader, Julius had an excellent memory. *Now, just where am I going to get the men to storm the main curtain wall gate?*

Despite his doubts, half an hour later, Constantine and Julius had managed to assemble seventy-five men for the operation.

"Centurion, you know the city best, so I want you to lead the charge," the tribune ordered. "I'll remain here with the rest of our men and the garrison to hold the fort, so to speak." Despite the quip, there was no humor left in the tribune's stance. He was determined, but tired, and his left hand was tightly wrapped in a bandage. But the fingers poking from the bandages still moved, and his face showed not a hint of pain.

I guess royalty still has some steel in their spines, Julius thought as he saluted. "You want me to retake the main city gate with seventy-five men, sir?" he asked again. He remembered passing through the imposing steel gates, with their stone towers stretching ten stories tall.

"General Minnicus has ordered us to retake the gate in preparation for the arrival of the rest of the legions. If we don't retake it, we can't get reinforcements. We've got support from units of the city garrison, but we'll have to get to them through streets that are still in control of rioters. So I leave the choice of routes up to you. Captain Alexandros will be supporting you with heavy weapons fire."

The tribune handed Julius a map of eastern Brittenburg. "He has also been kind enough to send down this street map indicating the streets he's certain are blocked." Julius looked at it. Almost half the roads were crossed out in red ink. Constantine's finger tapped the symbol identifying the main gate. "It's possible that enemy forces have gained control of the gate. We know for certain they have gained control of the two nearest towers." His finger circled the towers on either side of the gate complex. "This could mean the gate is in enemy hands, or it could mean the gate is in our hands, but we can't communicate with it. The Laurel flag still flies, but that could be a ruse. Keep your eyes open, but you must take that gate."

The tribune placed his hand on Julius's shoulder. "Don't doubt yourself. You know this city inside and out. The key to leadership is to lead by giving smart orders and not losing your cool, and I've already seen that in you, last night."

Julius nodded. Setting his shoulders, he met Constantine's eyes. "You can count on us, sir."

Constantine gave a grim smile. "I'm going to return to the gate here on the governor's estate. I'll leave operations in your capable hands." He turned and left.

Julius spent the next half-hour assembling his men and going over the route they were going to take. It was only a twenty-minute march away, assuming no roadblocks or other interruptions. He planned to seize the northern tower after picking up some garrison remnants supposedly holed up in a temple about halfway between the governor's mansion and their objective.

He formed his demi-cohort up, and they left the relative safety of the estate and headed east. The streets were deserted, littered with paper and clothing and sometimes a dead body. Julius gave orders that any corpse should be moved gently to the side of the street and treated with as much dignity as possible. This was his city; he was not going to debauch it further. The pace of his march slowed somewhat, but Julius refused to contradict his original orders.

A wave from a scout brought the column to a halt. "Two minutes rest," he told his men before advancing slowly over the broken cobblestones to the scout waiting at the corner of a building.

"Marcus, what do we have?"

"Look in those buildings over that way, right in front of that barricade across the street," the scout said, pointing toward the corner.

Julius doffed his helmet and peeked around the corner. "Second building from the left, sir," Marcus advised.

Julius watched for a moment. He saw the slightest of movements, and focused on that. "They've got a heavy repeater in that shop!" he exclaimed. Although the shadows did a good job of hiding the war machine, they had not concealed the telltale shine from the metal components.

"How would you like to deal with it? We can go around, but it would add a chunk of time." *Or we can go through it,* the scout had left unsaid. He was an experienced member of the legions, and was not as naïve as most of the rest of his men, Julius assumed.

"Have you spotted any more enemies? Do we even know if they are enemies?" Julius asked. The scout shook his head slowly, probably wondering if the new centurion wanted him to sign his own death warrant. Sensing his confusion, Julius explained himself. "Just wondering. I figured you're the best scout we have, Marcus, so you'd be the one to get the closest and figure out exactly who those people are. Wait here a moment, and I'll be back."

Turning, Julius entered one of the hole-in-the-wall shops that graced this street. A clothing shop, as it happened. The bell on the door jingled as he entered. The store appeared deserted. Julius helped himself to a men's white shirt hanging on a display rack, then dismantled the rack. A moment's work left him with a jury-rigged white flag.

Boots crunching on broken glass, Julius ducked low and returned to Marcus, now crouched behind a nearby cart. The scout was using a bit of mirror to try to see inside the window down the street. "No luck," Marcus said as Julius stopped behind him. He turned and watched the centurion drop his helmet and shrug off his scarlet centurion's cape.

Julius held the makeshift white flag beyond the cart, then slowly rose and moved toward the barricade, staying behind cover as much as possible.

"Halt!" a voice called out in Latin. "Do not move another step." Julius could detect no trace of accent. It definitely belonged to a Brittenburg man. Whether he was loyalist or rebel, Julius couldn't tell. "Who are you?" the voice demanded when Julius stopped.

"I'm a member of the XIII Germania Legion," Julius stated. He waited for a response, but none came.

Finally, the unknown voice came back with, "And what proof do we have that you are a loyal Roman? We've had far too many imposters."

Julius thought for a moment. How could he convince them that he was a loyalist? An idea popped into his head.

"You see that airship overhead? I can communicate with that. Whatever the rebels have done, they haven't got into our air fleet yet."

This answer set off a prolonged round of verbal fireworks behind the barricade. *Too many chiefs ...* Julius thought of their vague leadership as he inched closer. Finally he was close enough to climb over the barrels and burnt out motor trolley components forming the barricade. Julius stopped and glanced back. Marcus had retreated to the rest of the cohort and they had formed up in the street behind him, shields touching, prepared to back their seemingly fearless leader. Julius started climbing the barrier. He reached the top and found half a dozen repeater crossbows leveled at him.

"What are you doing here?" a dark-skinned man asked, his brown eyes bulging in alarm at the sudden appearance of the fully armored legionary officer. He wore the blue uniform of the auxilia and a dented brass helmet.

Julius held up his mailed hand. "Stop. I am Centurion Julius Brutus Caesar of the XIII Germania. Either you men are traitors, or you are loyal to the Empire. Decide now, before the thousand men of my legion crush your pitiful force beneath their heels." He glared at the dozen or so men before him. They were a mismatched lot. Without the identical albeit faded blue uniforms, it would have been hard to distinguish these men from a group of street toughs. The dark-skinned man gulped, and hastily ordered his men to lower their weapons.

Hiding his relief, Julius said, "Now, first things first." He gave the All Clear signal to the force behind him. The cohort switched from battle lines to loose column. As they began to stream up the street and over the barricade, Julius turned back to the dark-skinned man. "Are you the remnants of the city garrison that we were sent here to link up with?"

The leader nodded, then pulled off his helmet and ran his hand over his sweaty skull. He was older than Julius, maybe in his early thirties, but the lines of dirt and grime on his face made him look much older. "I'm Auxilia Centurion Druvic.

We're all that's left. We held off a wave of those rioters a while ago, and I lost three-quarters of my men." He looked over Julius's shoulder at the last of the legionnaires coming over the wall. "Is that all of you? Thought you had a thousand men with you." He turned bewildered eyes back to Julius.

Julius gave a weak smile. "Like I said, the legion does. We're only the 13th Cohort. Now, can you get us onto the wall? We must take the eastern gate to let the rest of the men inside."

"Of course, sir. Right this way." Druvic pointed down the street.

Off the demi-cohort walked, now joined by the remnants of the city garrison. For the first time, Julius felt as though they actually had a chance to save his city.

A shower of bolts thudded into the door of the mechanist's workshop. Julius ducked back behind the scant protection it offered. Several other men crouched in the darkened workshop, out of view. Julius peeked around the door again, this time finally getting a good angle on the tower.

One of many wall towers that had been taken by the rebels, either through assault or through subterfuge, had kept his cohort pinned down for the last hour. Julius could see that the lowest gate had been blown open, and he knew that was the only way in. The blockhouse defending the eastern gate was tightly closed, unwilling to open up for anyone. *If those idiots would stop pretending to be neutral and do their duty, we wouldn't have to storm this fricking tower,* he grumbled as another bolt leapt from the tower and hit an adjacent shop building. A high-pitched screaming started up, followed by a cry of "Medic!"

A medic with a red caduceus on his breastplate slid up beside Julius. "S'cuse me, Centurion," he mumbled as he brusquely pushed past and sprinted to the next building over. The tower fired several shots at him, but the medic slid into the safety of the building just in time.

Julius turned to the men behind him. "Gwendyrn, I've got an idea. We need doors, buckets, metal plates, and as many ropes as you can wrangle up. If we can't get them to leave the tower, we'll have to make them leave it."

A few hours later, the engineering-minded men of the demi-cohort had created a masterpiece. Without access to a steam engine, they had constructed a manual siege caterpillar using wrenches, hammers, and a few other tools at their disposal. Essentially a movable shed to cover an assault team and gate-breaking equipment, this one was made from layered doors and sheet metal. Combined, it was long enough to cover the entire demi-cohort. While about half the men held up the defensive shell, the rest would hold their shields on the sides, forming the rest of the caterpillar.

"Well, this is the best-looking siege equipment I've ever seen," Julius said. He was being honest, as he had never seen a real, active siege piece in his life. Not unless the ones on the propaganda posters counted. The engineers had constructed the caterpillar in three pieces, so that the few light artillery pieces they had could be hidden inside the caterpillar. Whenever a gap formed between the sections, the scorpions and heavy repeaters could provide covering fire for the advancing cohort.

"Load up!" Julius ordered.

Men rushed to their positions. Artillery crews manhandled their gear into their marching slots.

"Gwendyrn, I want you to take charge of the third section. You've got the ten-pound ballistae; try to knock out their weaponry. Auxilia Centurion Druvic will take the second segment. Let's move fast, gentlemen; we have to take this tower and retake that gate, and we should have had that done yesterday!" He yelled as he took his place under the first caterpillar section. The men cheered.

The siege pieces began to move forward toward the shattered opening at the base of the wall where the door used to be. They had to move around debris in the street, so it looked as though the segments were slithering toward the tower.

~ * * * ~

Up in the tower, the rebel commander was concerned. He had taken the tower through first treachery, then assault. A member of the garrison had been convinced to disable the tower weapons before opening the door, but a conscientious guard had killed the man before he'd completed his assignment. They'd succeeded in storming the tower, but those blasted loyalists were still trying to retake it. And now he was running low on ammunition.

Knowing the importance of the tower, the rebel commander sent half his force down to the main level to deal with the approaching caterpillar while keeping the rest in reserve. The men tramped down the stairs or took the central elevator down to the first floor. They armed themselves with captured repeater crossbows and took cover behind positions facing the entrance. There they waited, while the improvised Roman caterpillar moved closer. When the siege crawler was about fifty feet from their objective, the men hidden inside the tower's dark interior unleashed their bolts.

Cranggggg!

Screams and shouts came from the siege walker. Even with their thick shields between the legionnaires and the bolts, some of the projectiles still managed to find their marks. The rebels reloaded and aimed again.

~ * * * ~

The initial wave of bolts had been like the first lightning strike of a thunderstorm. One man in the lead caterpillar took a shaft through the eye as he adjusted his shield; he dropped, creating a gap in the formation. As the second rank struggled to get a man into the space, another wave of bolts prompted more screams and cries of alarm. A third wave, and the green legionnaires were faltering in the face of such deadly fire. Julius and the under-officers shouted orders to steady them while tightening up their formation.

Back in the third crawler, Gwendyrn saw the first taking punishing hits from the tower. "Hold up, men," he called out. "It's time we paid those rebels back with this baby." He patted the ten-pound ballista being pushed along beside him by several men. Behind them, other men pulled the small ammunition sled for the sleek machine. "Let's give our lads some supporting fire, shall we?"

The artillery crew quickly hauled their weapon into position; the rest of the men under the third siege caterpillar formed around it, protecting it while the crew assembled the destructive device. Only a few bolts were launched at them from the tower; the defenders were concentrating on decimating the closest siege engines.

Finally, the gunner cranked back the holder and the loader placed the explosive projectile into the groove. The gunner raised his hand.

"Step out!" called Gwendyrn. The men in front quickly sidestepped, leaving an opening for the weapon to shoot through.

The artillery commander adjusted his charge, aiming down the crosshair sights to adjust for distance, then fired. The wires vibrated with a distinct *tunggg*, throwing a black sphere through the air. In a beautiful shot that would go down in the XIII Germania's annals, the explosive sailed over the defenders, through the shattered base of the tower, and detonated. Red and yellow flames shot from the dark opening, accompanied by a wave of shrapnel and a brief drizzle of red liquid and body parts. Screams and shouts echoed faintly over the sizzle of the flames against the steel and stone walls.

Seeing the destruction, the men in the first caterpillar raised their explosive plumbatae and launched a second, devastating blast of explosives at the defenders, wreaking more havoc. Gwendyrn watched as the centurion's men charged, eager to dish out some retribution on the remaining rebels. Finally dropping the protection of the siege crawler, they ran forward at full speed, hacking down any enemy survivors. A short time later, a single figure waved his hand at the other caterpillars.

Mustering his men, Gwendyrn ordered them forward to join their comrades at the foot of the tower.

~ * * * ~

Julius led his men three abreast through the large opening at the base of the tower. Low fires smoldered inside, barely illuminating the large, dimly lit space and casting looming shadows over the blackened walls. Men cursed as they tripped over unseen objects on the ground. Julius called for a light, any light, to show the way. Finally a legionnaire brought forward a scavenged lantern, and Julius turned it up to full strength—revealing a charnel house. Dead men and dismembered body parts lay everywhere. The smell of death hung heavily over the place. Several men began to dry heave. Wiping his own mouth and taking a drink of water to settle his stomach, Julius pushed his men onward, thinking, *I'm fortunate I don't have much left to give.* The longer they stayed in this place, the worse it would get.

Moving quickly now, the first demi-cohort charged up the tower stairs. Foot by foot, the 13th Cohort fought its way up the tower. Each floor became a miniature battlefield as they went toe to toe with the remaining rebels. Several of the legionnaires began using plumbatae warheads to help clear the rooms by unscrewing the warhead, quickly opening a door and chucking the warhead as hard as possible inside, and ducking back, hoping that the warhead would detonate.

The last bastion of resistance succumbed after a desperate sword fight, with new centurion Julius leading the way. Although not a sword master, Julius at least had the rudiments down. His opponent, apparently the leader of the rebels, was a thin man who handled a broadsword like he'd never used one before; in fact, he looked almost incapable of hefting the large weapon. Julius advanced on him as his companions spread out, taking the fight to the enemy.

Surprising Julius, the leader ducked behind a ballista, heaving it around toward the oncoming men. *Tunnngg!* The machine bucked, but the untrained rebels had forgotten to load the weapon. Abandoning the artillery piece, the man advanced, swinging his sword at Julius, who took the blow on his raised shield. The sword sank several inches into the wood and steel, the force of it nearly wrenching the safeguard out of his hands. Arm numb, Julius backpedaled, avoiding another swing.

The man flailed away at him, taking large, predictable swings that were quickly tiring him. A glance around confirmed for Julius that the rebels were all but eliminated. A moment later, the last vestiges of resistance crumbled as the few men left fled onto the battlements.

"Give over, man, it's done," Julius called to the leader.

The rebel grunted and wiped sweat off his brow before hefting his massive sword once more. "I'm dead either way," he growled, and charged.

Julius parried, ducked another blow, then stabbed with his sword as he had been taught in basic training. Short, chopping strokes drove the man back one more time, until Julius got right in his face with his shield, pressed forward, and sliced. The sword slid across the man's chest. Dark red blood welling from the deep gash, he collapsed, sword clanging onto the metal grating beside him.

Trembling, Julius took a deep breath. He cleaned his sword on the dying man's tunic, whispering a hasty apology. Sheathing his sword, he looked up to see Gwendyrn's squads arriving.

"Didn't leave any for us?" Gwendyrn asked, looking around.

"There are plenty left, if those other gate towers are held by the rebels. Take your men along the wall. I'm going to try to get in touch with headquarters. It seems the rebels were using the wireless set here in the tower," Julius replied. "My tech man was killed; do you have someone who can work it?"

"First sending my men out to do the dirty work, now stealing my techie. Instead of senior centurion, perhaps your title should be senior delegator?"

Gwendyrn had stepped over the line. The mood in the room cooled, as men turned to watch the confrontation between their officers. Sensing the mood shift, both Julius and Gwendyrn stared at one another. Julius held the panic inside his heart in a tight grip, refusing to let it show on his face. Finally, the junior centurion twitched as a bead of sweat trickled down his temple. Gwendyrn blinked.

"Well, if you're too lazy to go over and figure out what's happening at the gate, I suppose I can find one of my men to lead your squads for you, *Junior Centurion*," Julius said. "Perhaps you will be one of those men, if you cannot find the *courage* necessary to lead your men." The challenge hung in the air, with only the sounds of distant fighting providing a soundtrack to the tension in the room.

Gwendyrn finally spoke, the words sounding as though they were dragged from the pit of his stomach. "No need to get all testy, *sir*, I'll lead them." He jerked a thumb back at one of his men. "Klautus here will help you contact the tribune." He gave a sloppy salute. "By your leave, sir, I'll be taking my men out."

Julius calmly saluted with perfect precision, and watched Gwendyrn's face color slightly. "Good luck, Centurion Gwendyrn."

As Gwendyrn turned and ordered his men out of the room onto the battlements, Julius turned to the rest of his men. "Secure the tower, round up any weapons, dispose of the dead, and place a guard on the ground floor. I want to initiate contact with the remnants of the garrison up here. And get some men on these weapons!" He pointed to the heavy artillery pieces.

Men scrambled to follow his orders. He turned to Legionnaire Klautus. "Follow me. I want to get this wireless set up and running."

The room was chaotic for the next few minutes as men tramped up and down the stairs, carrying bodies down and fresh supplies up. One man found the red and green flag of the Empire and raised it on the flagpole.

Julius found himself lightheaded for a moment as the entirety of the situation crashed down upon him. He had led men, ordered the deaths of an entire group of enemy fighters, including citizens of his own city, and now he felt proud? How could he feel this?

He climbed the ladder up to the observation deck and took several shaky steps over to the city side, looking out across the panorama of the city. *His city*. Pulling out his expensive "borrowed" binoculars—the owner of the fine optics shop had deserted his building and even forgot to lock up— he aimed them at Sludge Bottom. He fiddled with the dials, even finding a setting that let him see possible heat signatures in some buildings—*That's useful*—but it was no help. A heavy pall of dark smoke and fog lay over the entire western portion of the city. The Nortland airship was bobbing in and out of the smoke, engaging in a cat and mouse game with the smaller *Scioparto*.

Sighing, he tucked the binoculars back into their padded case and secured it carefully to his belt. From a small pouch he withdrew a pocket watch and flipped it open to regard his sister's picture, on the inside lid. He closed his eyes for a moment.

A short cough pulled him from his thoughts. Legionnaire Klautus stood behind him. "Sir, I've got the wireless working. But before you contact base, you may want to hear this."

Julius nodded that he should continue.

"Centurion Gwendyrn reports that the gate garrison has opened their doors and acknowledge your authority over them. The main gates have been opened as per your instructions."

Julius leapt for joy, the bristles of his helmet scraping the ceiling. "Yes! Alright, get that message off quick to the tribune. He will definitely be happy to hear that."

"Sir, look!" called a lookout. Julius turned to see him pointing at the gate towers. From each one a long, flowing Imperial flag had been dropped to hang against the dark walls. Julius extracted his binoculars again and trained them across to the other towers. All along the wall, the formerly neutral tower wardens were flying imperial flags.

Julius beamed. All of a sudden, those long odds didn't appear to be quite so impossible as before.

~ * * * ~

The long red line wound through the eastern gate into the contested city. Julius watched from above the main gatehouse, eyelids heavy with exhaustion. His men had held the gatehouse and neighboring towers for the last two days against several enemy assaults. They had been left without air cover the first day, as the *Scioparto* had departed to meet up with the train bringing the rest of the legion. Only the absence of fire from the enemy airship indicated that they had run out of bombs to use against the defenders. The *Scioparto* had returned on day two, bringing enough men to secure the governor's mansion and expand the grasp of the loyalist forces.

The reinforcements had joined in several pitched street battles fought around and along the route from the gate to the mansion until a corridor had been cleared and secured. A newfound respect and a growing sense of brotherhood was forming between the city garrison, the remaining constabulary forces, and the strengthened 13th Cohort. The effective strength of the 13th was rapidly doubling, even with the heavy casualties sustained during the street fighting.

Julius watched the XIII Germania continue at a measured pace into the city, passing the shells of burned out buildings, shattered war machines, and the aluminum skeleton of the Nortland airship as they moved up to the mansion. A young centurion walked out into the sunshine behind Julius. He put up a hand to shade his eyes from the bright noonday sun warming the stone and steel surface of the battlements.

An orderly squeezed around and brushed past him, murmuring a hasty "Excuse me, sir" as he approached Julius. "Centurion Caesar , sir, we've been ordered back to the mansion for refit and recovery time." Julius nodded without turning around. "Who is the gentleman with you, Latius?"

The other officer stepped up and cleared his throat. "Ah*em*. I'm Centurion Hortatus of the 4th Cohort, here to replace you at the eastern gate."

Julius nodded. "It's all yours, Centurion. Take good care of it. Loyal men fought and died for this gate," he said solemnly, turning to look at the new officer.

Hortatus blanched. "You look as though you've aged fifteen years," he blurted, then colored at the indiscretion.

Julius brought a hand up to the mass of congealed blood concealing a gash on his cheek, a souvenir from a close encounter with an enemy sword. He had no idea what he looked like, but if his face were any mirror of his fatigue, he imagined he looked like hell. Wordlessly, Julius turned and walked out of the sunshine into the dark interior of the tower, his orderly following behind him.

"Gather the men; we're leaving here," he ordered. The aide scurried off. Julius took a deep breath and leaned on a borrowed plumbata. Weariness had soaked into every bone in his body. He brushed away an imaginary speck of dust on his shoulder. His nose wrinkled as he smelled himself. *Ugh, I need a bath. That would feel absolutely amazing right now.* Looking around, Julius sighed. *Guess there's no chance of a bath or even a hot shower anywhere around here.*

The thud of boots on the cobblestones behind him piqued his interest. Earlier, he would have drawn his sword in a flash, challenging any would-be intruder or rebel. Now he merely turned slightly, hand going to his belt but not even reaching the hilt of his sword.

The survivors of his demi-cohort were arriving. Julius formed them up, getting them into a … partial … formation. The young centurion knew better than to try to force these men into neat, orderly rows. Besides, he just didn't care.

"Good job, men, you have surpassed all expectations. You are true Romans," he said in a quiet voice. The men nodded, some attempting to salute with tired arms. Julius jerked his head, and his men moved out.

~ * * * ~

A short time later, the 13th Cohort was reunited in the main hall of the governor's mansion. Tribune Appius stood waiting for his men, having been informed of their impending arrival by an eager messenger boy who had sprinted all the way to the great hall from the main gate. Outside, the bones of a new legion fort were going up in the estate gardens. The sound of hammers slowly stilled and, like the men who drifted over to silently watch the battle-weary legionaries, Constantine moved to a window to witness their arrival. He was shocked at the ragged look of his men. They did not look like the green demi-cohort that had been deployed less than seventy-two hours prior. They were a battle-hardened, veteran detachment.

When they were only a couple of meters away, Constantine heard Centurion Caesar order, "Company, sal*ute*." Ignoring their weariness, the survivors crisply saluted their commanding officer.

For the first time in his life, the tribune felt a stirring in his breast, an extra pounding of his heart. Without thought, his hand came up in a smart salute. All around him, the men in the hall snapped to attention, regardless of uniform or connection. The young heir lowered his hand, overwhelmed by events.

"Dismissed!" cried his new centurion. The men fell out, moving off in pairs and trios, many helped by combat medics toward the hospital wing. The centurion strode across the beautiful marble floors inlaid with intricate metal spirals and mosaics made of different metals and gears until he stood next to his commanding officer.

"Good job, Centurion Caesar . Your mission was a success. Would you say your men are ready for another mission?" the tribune asked. Julius nodded hesitantly. "We've been busy while you were gone. The general wants to see us. Seems he has an even grander plan for our newfound talents."

Seeing Julius's lips tighten and his eyes narrow, Constantine offered a wan smile. "No worries, that's tomorrow. Today, go get some hot grub and some sleep." He sniffed. "And definitely find a new uniform somewhere. I think you'll have to burn that one."

CHAPTER

13

G ENERAL MINNICUS SLAMMED HIS POINTER down near the miniature representation of the seaward curtain wall. "You will take the fight to them, Tribune, and we will take this city back from those imbeciles who dare rebel against our *Imperial authority!*"

Through his contacts in the capital, Constantine had heard that his father had given Minnicus permission to torture and execute any rebel he came across. In addition, Minnicus was also given the rights to any capture rebel's *property*. Which, Constantine thought, might lead to a conflict of interest. He resolved to keep a closer eye on the newly ambitious general.

The large man leaned over the table, his automatic arm coming to rest with a hiss and slight whine next to him. He moved several small figures amongst the shining copper buildings and avenues. "You will lead your cohort, with the 7th, 9th, and 11th in support, up the western Via Germania, through the slums here." The telescoping pointer tapped the darker mass of buildings representing Sludge Bottom. He looked around at Constantine and the cohort commanders' faces. The men all looked pointedly at the three-dimensional map, waiting for the general to continue.

Finally the thin baton tapped another point in the miniature city. "You will then ascend the curtain wall here, against the seaward side. Scouts report that there is considerable scaffolding there due to wall maintenance. You will use this scaffolding to gain access to the battlements, bypassing the towers. From there, you will take these towers." Minnicus shifted slightly, and his arm whined as a piston gradually compacted. "The 7th and 9th will take the southern tower, while the 11th and 13th take the northern tower." Finished, he leaned back on his three-legged stool.

Centurion Dryx of 7th Cohort raised a hand. Minnicus nodded. "Sir, what is the goal of this mission?"

Several other officers visibly tensed, noting the unspoken reasons for this question. On the surface, it looked like a suicide mission. Send five hundred men deep into a hostile city to scale walls and take defended positions?

Minnicus glowered at the freckle-faced centurion. "The goal is to take those towers. They have air defense mounted ballista and heavy scorpions that were reportedly undamaged in the initial assault. The troops manning those towers deserted or turned to the enemy. By taking those defenses, we eliminate the rebels' ability to get supplies from the Nortlanders. In addition, the last remaining air pad controlled by the rebels is right between those two towers. Once you take those defenses, I want you to knock out the last airship. Bad winds have slowed our air fleet coming from Britannia, so we're on our own."

The general held out his hand and a silent servant placed a glass of wine into it. He heavily, then smacked his lips and looked around. "Any more questions?" Seeing no response, he stood. "Tribune Appius of the 13th will take the lead on this one. His cohort is the most blooded of ours."

The officers stood at attention while the general left the command room, flunkies dogging his heels. As the tent flap fell shut behind him, blocking out the sun, someone muttered, "By the gods, I suppose we should get our wills up to date."

Constantine moved closer to the table. He leaned over, tracing their route with his finger. "Not yet. I have a few ideas. We'll complete our objectives, but we'll do it my way. No need to lose our arms over it." The other men couldn't help but smile at the underhanded jab at the departed general. "This is what I need us to get ahold of first ..."

~ * * * ~

The men of the 11th and 13th Cohorts moved in two single files on either side of the cobblestone street. Looming buildings crowded out the morning sun, and the streets were dark and murky. Every small noise or slight movement ratcheted up the level of anxiety in the column.

They had been awakened before daybreak, and wrapped their boots with rags to muffle the noise of their passing. They had gathered their things and departed in the inky pre-dawn, separating into two divisions. The 11th and 13th Cohorts were making their way toward the northern tower #23 on the western wall, while the 7th and 9th Cohorts targeted the southern tower, #22.

Almost immediately the southern cohorts ran into trouble. A small group of rebel saboteurs were lucky (or perhaps, unlucky) enough to be preparing an ambush in several buildings when the first legionnaires emerged from the mists right before them. Both parties hesitated a few moments, shocked at the appearance of the other. Then the first few legionnaires recovered and pulled out their swords to charge their surprised foes. A few more competent members of the ragtag militia responded in kind. Steel met steel, the sound echoing down the empty streets, though the dense fog dampened most of the reverberations of combat. Blood joined dew on the cold streets, pooling to run slowly in channels toward the sewers.

Although the fight was brief, it had destroyed the secrecy of the operation. His cover blown, the commanding tribune of the 7th and 9th Cohorts ordered his men forward, determined to reach the wall before losing the fog cover.

From far off, Corbus heard the short clash of metal, the yelling, then silence. He knelt and looked down the cobblestone street, his brown cloak settling onto the damp paving stones around him as his troop waited, armed and armored, behind him. Bracing himself with one hand, he leaned far forward and turned his head to press a cheek against the wet cobbles. Closing his eyes, he *focused* deep inside himself, then stretched his senses out to the narrow streets and dilapidated tenements around him.

Thumpthumpthumpthumpthumpthump ...

"What do you hear, My Lord?" asked his second in command, Xersia. He had moved up to stand next to his oddly situated leader. The fog had settled as condensation on his flat-brimmed steel helmet, and it dripped onto the collar of his blue cloak.

Corbus leaned back and turned to look at Xersia. His reflection stared back at him from the man's burnished breastplate. "We're about to have company. Warm up the engines, but keep them at low power. Let's prepare a warm reception for our visitors. Quietly—I don't want them to be prepared for our little surprise party."

Xersia nodded and turned, directing squads to the prepared defenses with little more than a grunt and a wave of his wicked serrated dagger.

Corbus rose and stretched his arms and legs with controlled, precise movements. He slid a set of double swords from their sheaths on his back. His men assigned to their stations, Xersia pulled out an apple and bit into it, then made a face and spit out the chunk. He examined the apple. "Rotten," he muttered.

Without stopping his warm-up, Corbus said, "Thought someone as rotten as you would like rotten apples."

Grinning, Xersia chucked the rotten apple at his commander.

Swish, then *swack*—a flurry of motion—*swish*. The apple, now sliced into six pieces, fell to the street.

Xersia grunted and nodded approvingly. "Good."

Corbus eyed him.

"Swords make things too fancy." Xersia pulled a massive chain-axe over his shoulder. Holding it one-handed, an impressive feat of strength, he placed it against the largest piece of apple remaining on the ground. A calloused thumb clicked the activator. The minute engine inside the axe whined to life, and the small, serrated teeth started moving, making applesauce of the apple core. He grinned at Corbus.

The assassin smiled back. "Have I mentioned how happy I am that we're working *together* on this mission?"

A few minutes later, the hapless 7th and 9th Cohorts from the XIII Germania appeared through the fog, individual legionnaires solidifying from ghostlike shapes into detailed men as they approached the rebels' ambush position.

A massive construct lumbered out of a mist-shrouded side street, dew glinting on long steel tusks and an articulated trunk. The retrofitted mechaniphant seemed to shake off the condensation as it approached. Fustus, the gangleader in command, put his wrists together and twined his thumbs, then turned the hand signal elbows-up in an inverted sign of the Aquila, indicating "death of the empire." A surprisingly realistic imitation of an elephant's trumpet erupted from the mechaniphant's mechanical speakers as it bowled appalled legionnaires over like pins. Corbus joined in the cheer from his men as they fell upon the hapless cohorts.

The slaughter commenced.

~ * * * ~

Squinting down at his map, Constantine remembered, for about the tenth time, that he needed to go to the speculafabricor for a new pair of specs. Rubbing at the bridge of his nose, he stared around at the all-encompassing fog, then checked his chromation. Almost eight o'clock! The fog should be burning off soon. No sooner had that thought popped into his head than he felt the first gust of a sea breeze pushing its way through the fog. It whistled down the alleys and side streets, bringing the sounds of battle to his ears. Constantine cocked his head, listening. Should he try to divert his men from their path to assist their comrades? Or should they push on? He stood between the two columns of men, pondering, when a legionnaire ran up to him, and his choice was suddenly made for him.

"Sir, we've reached the wall. It appears ... well, it appears empty, sir. May Zeus strike me down, but I'd swear there were no defenders!" The soldier appeared as surprised with this good turn of events as Constantine was.

There was no stopping the advance now. If his men could take the wall unopposed, they could take their objective and go to the aid of their compatriots.

Constantine jogged forward to the front of the line. Men were gathering around the scaffolding, while several scouts moved up the haphazard construction. Looking up at the incredibly high wall, Constantine wondered what they would find once they reached the top.

Centurion Hoagar, from the 11th Cohort, waved a greeting as he worked his way through his idle men, bellowing, "Make way there, I say, make way! You, you, and you—detail some men to watch our flanks and rear. Don't want to be ambushed while climbing a ruddy great staircase!" Squad leaders gave orders and several files of men marched to the rear.

Julius approached. "Sir, what are your orders? Do you want us to push ahead? Scouts indicate that the way is clear."

The tribune tilted his head and gave this several minutes' thought. The centurion wet his lips, preparing to probe for a response, but Constantine spoke first. "The 13th will take the lead. The 11th will remain here in support. Once the 13th has secured the battlement, we'll signal the go-ahead," He pointed to a large cargo elevator hidden behind an iron framework. "We'll use that to bring up the 11th faster. But *we're* going to have to take the stairs. Prepare the men for a hike."

As Julius saluted and marched away, a messenger ran up. "We're ready to move, sir. Eleventh Cohort has taken defensive positions and the scouts have pushed ahead. We're just awaiting your Go order."

Constantine nodded, and followed the messenger back to the main body of men. He ordered them forward, into the dense maze of wood and steel scaffolding. It was like moving through tunnels—heavy cloth was draped on the city side to prevent men or material from falling through; opposite lay the slick steel wall, pitted here and there with rust that was constantly being cleaned out and painted over with rust-resistant paint. The scaffolding zigged and zagged; at the end of each level, they would ascend to the next via a steep ramp. As the men scrabbled up each level, their pace slowed. Even Constantine found the climbing tedious and repetitive: wall on the left, canvas on the right; wall on the right, canvas on the left.

He paused for a moment to push aside the heavy canvas covering for a view of the city. The fog was almost gone, and he could clearly see the once beautiful city now marred by fire, smoke, and destruction. He called the column to a halt. "Take five minutes, rehydrate and check your equipment," he ordered. "Centurion and squad leaders, on me."

All along the column, tired men sat, leaning against walls and taking long drinks from canteens. The officers of the 13th Cohort assembled in a half-circle around their leader as he sketched out his plan.

"When we hit that battlement, I want half our men going in each direction. Julius, you take first through fifth squads left, pushing and holding south." Julius nodded, as those squad leaders looked at him, Gwendyrn among them. "I'll take the rest of the cohort north, along with the scout auxilia squad. Secure the landing area on the wall if you can, prevent the enemy from using it if you can't. We'll take the northern tower. Questions?"

Silence from the officers, accompanied by several shaken heads. Then a raised hand. "Sir, what if the other cohorts don't show up to reinforce?" asked the taciturn head of third squad, Gravus.

Constantine narrowed his eyes in thought. "We'll just have to do the work ourselves. *Audeamus* to take our objectives without the support we were promised. General Minnicus will grind his teeth at that one." At several quizzical looks, Constantine sighed. "'Let us dare!' Do none of you men speak High Latin?"

The officers looked at each other. Julius piped up. "I would hazard to say that our High Latin is a bit rusty, sir. Public schooling doesn't instill much High Latin. Unless you're recitin' a prayer, we won't be able to understand it."

Constantine frowned. "Very well, *alea iacta est*. Gather the men; they've had enough break time. It's time to crush some rebel scum." He paused as he saw the look of confusion on their faces again. Exasperated, he explained, "The dice have been cast, men; don't any of you remember Julius Caesar?" The men all turned to look at their centurion. Shaking his head, Constantine pulled off his helmet and rubbed his short-cropped hair. "The *Emperor*, Savior of the Republic and my ancestor, you idiots. Come on, now." He pushed past them, hearing a few snickers from those nearby.

"The die's been cast?" he overheard Gwendyrn muttering to Centurion Caesar . "Didn't know the tribune was a betting man. Hopefully he won't go spouting off any more of that High Latin garbage in battle. Won't be any time for a translation."

"Well, Gweny," the centurion responded, "I think that there is more to that man than meets the eye, even if he is a high-up muckety-muck." Julius's gauntleted hand clanked against the other man's helmet. "Time to get to work."

Up and up the cohort climbed, until finally they arrived at the top. Looking left and right along the wall, Constantine saw only a few guards, but a mass of equipment and heavy artillery. Farther north, several crews were using heavy ballistae and scorpions to rain artillery fire down into the city. A medium-sized trebuchet was also in action, its arm whipping up with a clang and a low whoosh to hurl several explosive canisters out over the war-torn city. Their target appeared to be close to the wall farther south, where the sounds of fighting were more evident now.

Constantine looked at his men and met fierce, predatory faces looking back at him. "They aren't expecting us. Take them quickly, take them quietly. Remember, our goal is the tower. Soon enough it will be *us* raining fire down on *them!*" he said confidently, though it hid an inner nervousness. "Alright, men, divide up—move, move, move!"

Gathering the men, Centurion Caesar and Tribune Appius quickly divvied up their forces. Julius saluted Constantine.

"See you on the other side, Centurion," Constantine said.

"Don't make us come save your behind now, sir," the centurion chided.

~ * * * ~

Julius led his squads to the left. Almost immediately, several rebel guards noticed their approach. With a yell, Julius charged, his men on his heels. To the rebels, they looked like a wave of red, moving straight at them. Several of them panicked, threw down their weapons, and ran for their lives. Those few souls foolhardy enough to remain and fight were quickly dispatched. No Imperials were injured during the brief skirmish. Julius quickly set his men to work disposing of the bodies by tossing them over the wall into the sea, and securing the heavy weapons.

"Gods curse them," Julius muttered as the large gears on the cargo elevator stopped turning and the iron grills opened, disgorging several dozen heavily armed and armored brown-coated rebels farther down the walkway. The fleeing men had located reinforcements. "Shields up!" he shouted.

Scrambling into position, his men formed a human roadblock five men wide across the walkway. A few men threw together a barricade behind the line, creating a makeshift wall upon the wall.

The foe approached at a jog, led by a huge, screaming man wielding a massive axe. *Really?* Julius thought sardonically. *They still make barbarians in that mold?*

The two sides clashed as if two trains had hit each other at full speed. Shields shattered. Men tumbled backward. The giant was already through the first rank of men and into the second. Behind him, his men fought with the dazed remnants of the first line, fighting back to back now against the onslaught.

"Crossbows! Take them from behind!" Julius shouted at his rearmost men.

Some men climbed atop the parapet, trying to gain a higher vantage point from which to take shots at the enemy. Bolts whistled through the air, and two brown forms crumpled to the walkway. The enemy pressed forward, fighting to get out of the line of fire. Several hurled throwing axes in response, and one crossbowman fell from the battlements with a scream of pain. The Imperial line began to waver.

"Push them! Shields low and press them!" Julius shouted. "C'mon boys, push them forward! Remember your training! Stab and block, stab and block!" He shoved his way through the ranks to the front. Wide-eyed men glanced back at him as they struggled to hold off the unrelenting assault. Julius planned his next move carefully. "Fourth rank forward, third rank, retire!" he shouted, and the men before him fell back, trying to make room for their relief.

At the same moment, the giant Nortlander launched a new attack. A mighty swing of his axe shattered a man's shield. Pieces of steel-reinforced wood flew in all directions, mixed with gore. The unfortunate legionnaire collapsed, cradling the stump of his arm. With a cry of victory, the barbarian twirled his axe back into position, readying for the killing stroke.

Julius lowered his head and charged into the fray, taking the barbarian completely by surprise. Knocked off balance, the giant lost momentum, and Julius seized the advantage, bending low and pushing into the large man, thrusting his sword forward in short, lightning fast jabs. Parrying, the Nortlander chieftain fell back several feet. The two men eyed each other, shuffling this way and that, watching for an opening.

Legionnaires had dragged their injured comrade to safety behind the line. Fresh ranks moved up to cover their leader. The rebels formed their own line just a few yards away. Their leader turned and continued to exult his men in their harsh, Nordic language. Julius looked at his soldiers, gave an exaggerated nod, and abruptly charged.

The sudden assault shook their enemy, but they refused to break. *These are not rebels who happen to have a Nortland leader,* Julius realized. *They must all be Nortland raiders.* Shouts and yells washed over him as his men charged again. Shield to shield, sword to axe, the Imperials forced their opponents back toward the elevator and landing platform.

Julius stabbed again and again. His arm burned with fatigue and his shield arm tingled under the multitude of blows raining down upon it. Small cuts and nicks burned up and down his arms and he tasted blood in his mouth. Sword dripping blood, he backed out and let a fresh man take his place.

Farther down the line, a man collapsed with an axe through his *galea*, the steel helmet shattered by the force of the blow. Another legionnaire stepped up to take his place. The discipline of his men was beginning to tell. Their opponents were frustrated, unable to break through the now solid Imperial line.

With an ear-shattering bellow, the Nortland chieftain waded into the fray again. This time, the young centurion was ready for him. Watching the massive axe swing by, even as he felt the wind of its passing, Julius stabbed down at the Nortlander's unguarded left leg. His sword bit deep, penetrating chain mail and flesh before Julius twisted his sword and withdrew it.

The burly man stumbled, looked at his leg then, strangely unaffected by the hideous wound streaming blood, he turned toward Julius and flicked something on his axe. With a teeth-gritting screech, the edge of the axe began to move, speeding up until it was a steady blur.

"Watch out, he's got a chain-axe!" cried Calis, who had been guarding Julius's flank. While he stood frozen, amazed at the fortitude of the adversary before him, Calis was holding off two attackers moving in tandem, stretching the young legionnaire's skills. He barely avoided one blow, and blocked another. Another legionnaire ran up to help the beleaguered duo, and Julius advanced to meet the seemingly invincible giant for a third time.

The Nortlander leered at him. "Come, puny Roman, let us see what you've got. My axe thirsts for blood. *Your blood!*" he shouted in heavily accented Low Latin. Axe whirling, he advanced on the smaller man.

Julius gritted his teeth and, shield held across his body, circled his opponent, grasping for any way of avoiding a punishing hit from the weighted chain-axe. *It would go through my shield like a saw at a sawmill. If I can waste time, that wound of his will drain him of blood.*

While their men grappled on the battlements, the two leaders continued to jostle for position.

A wounded man's hand reached out and grasped Julius's ankle. He tugged and pulled, but the man wouldn't let go. With a wordless growl, Julius swung his sword, amputating the man's hand. In that critical second of distraction, the chieftain barreled into him, sending him flying against the stone and steel bulwark. Julius's vision clouded for a second. When it cleared, he saw his men throwing themselves at the oversized Nortlander, straining to keep themselves between their leader and his attacker. The axe killed, wounded, or forced them away one by one. Julius fumbled with his shield, using it to prop himself up against the parapet. His legs were shaking and his stomach wanted to empty itself.

"I hope you are ready, little Roman, to meet those gods you love so much." The colossus was right before him, gloating. With lightning speed, he swung his axe. Julius ducked just in time, feeling the weapon's passage like a heavy wind grabbing at his cloak. The base of the weapon connected with Julius's back, knocking the wind out of him again, while the strange keening sound became more and more muffled. His fingers grasped at his throat. His cloak was choking him! He moved his hands to work desperately at the clasp.

Finally the clasp sprang free, the cloak whisked away, and Julius straightened, wheezing. The chieftain still stood before him, now staring in angry confusion at his weapon. The deadly chain-axe mewled in fits and spurts, its teeth fouled up by the thick woolen cloak, which was now tightly wrapped around it.

Gripping his sword with both hands, Julius advanced. The Nortlander dropped the useless weapon and pulled out daggers, long brown hair waving wildly in the wind as he faced Julius. Out of nowhere, two steel bolts slammed into the man's chest, punching through his burnished breastplate. He staggered and nearly fell. Julius swung his sword up and brought it down with as much force as he could muster. The barbarian's head, sliced clean from his shoulders, tumbled to the ground. His body followed, landing with a crash that shook the parapet.

A brief pause followed as both sides stopped their conflict to gape at the fallen giant. Julius coughed. "Finish them off!" he ordered, struggling to push his voice above the sounds of battle.

Those remaining of the enemy fought on, powered by revenge and anger, but they were no match for superior Roman numbers and discipline. The last few threw down their swords, trying to surrender, but the Romans were in the grip of battle rage. There were no survivors.

The weary centurion turned to look at his savior, standing just a few feet away. Squad Leader Gwendyrn smiled, looking abashedly down at a pair of still quivering repeater crossbows. "I've been waiting for a chance to fire two of these at the same time."

CHAPTER

14

THE GEARS OF THE ELEVATOR squeaked and squealed as the engine pulled the cargo elevator slowly up the steep side of the curtain wall. Within, the last remaining members of the rebellion, along with their Nortland allies, prepared for battle. Word had come that the Imperial forces had surged up from a hidden access route along the wall, fighting their way toward the rebels' last remaining lifeline to the outside world. A company had already been sent ahead to deal with the attackers. The remaining forces had neatly eviscerated the first Roman assault with a well-placed ambush down below, and had now fallen back to eliminate this second assault.

Tucked into a corner of the elevator, Corbus and his mother held a brief conference. "I've contacted the Nortlanders, and they have their airship on the way. It should be close, but I figure we can hold off the Imperials for a while. We'll meet up with some more of our compatriots on the wall, and kick those Romans so hard they'll have wished they never crossed the Rhine!" Amalia finished with a wicked grin.

Corbus nodded, listening to his mother's plan while running a whetstone across his twin bluesteel blades. The quadruple-folded layers of rare metal created an impossibly sharp edge as well as incredible toughness. The weapon could bend and flex without developing weak spots or becoming brittle. Polishing and sharpening it was one of Corbus's pre-battle rituals.

Amalia looked at him and smiled. "Soon the day will come when the Romans lie dying in the streets, and we will lead the Germans back from the trashcan of history to trample and crush them," she said quietly, proudly. Then she closed her eyes. A strange keening rose from her throat as she started working herself into a battle trance, gripping the carved staff of her double-ended spear so tightly that her knuckles went white. Her facial muscles twitched with the barely contained battle madness, and she opened and closed her eyes without registering what she saw.

Corbus scooted away a bit, unnerved by the pseudo-mysticism component of her warrior side, and raised his voice. "Friends, let us prepare ourselves. We have companions awaiting us on the wall, ready to help us reach safety. Each one of you is an asset to the cause. Do not waste your life needlessly. I will take the lead. Remember our goal above all else. Get to the transport. We are the seed of the future. If we die, our children, and their children, forever and beyond, will be shackled to the wheel of industry and corruption that is Rome." The men nodded, knowing the challenge that awaited them.

The elevator hissed as it reached the top level, releasing small wisps of steam that the wind from the bay tugged along with it. Corbus grasped the handles of the wicker door and slid it aside. His men poured out, quickly finding cover from which to assess the situation.

Corbus watched from his vantage point as the last few survivors of the first company were slaughtered at the hands of the victorious Romans. He cursed under his breath.

Amalia appeared next to him. "By the furies, how did they reach here so fast?" she asked.

Boots pounded across the concrete behind him—the last of his men had arrived from a hatchway. "Did you activate

Operation Vindicator?" she inquired of their leader. The file leader nodded nervously.

Corbus pulled out his pocket chromation and studied the hands behind the fogged glass for a moment before showing it to his mother. "We don't have much time to waste, then."

"We have plenty of time to dispatch these enemies of freedom," Amalia hissed.

Nodding, Corbus turned to his men. "Volley fire, crossbows, on my order."

Up and down the wall, his men were loading and cocking their weapons, aiming at the Romans now reforming farther along the wall toward the northern tower. An alert soldier pointed at the motley assortment of guerillas and mercenaries and shouted a warning just as they finished loading their weapons.

Corbus's sword flicked out. "Shoot!" he yelled, sweeping the sword down. The miniature storm of bolts flashed toward the Romans, catching them unawares. Without time to form a decent shield wall, the volley devastated them. A dozen men fell writhing in pain, while others stood motionless. The officer in charge tried frantically to regain control over his surprised men, and they stumbled into formation, placing their large *scuta* in front of them. The sun broke through the departing fog and clouds to reflect off the central metal bosses of their shields.

"Corbus, you get the men out, I'll keep them at bay!" Amalia shouted as the remaining Romans began to advance on their position, shield wall preventing the rebel missiles from doing any more damage. Corbus felt rather than saw his mother move past him, her warrior essence nearly flowing into battle. Spear angled low, she charged the Roman line with a piercing wail that drove shards of ice into his soul and made his hands move involuntarily to cover his ears. The Romans nearly broke right there, but for the opposing officer waving his sword frantically and shouting encouraging words to his men. Corbus could just hear the faint exultations over his mother's blood-curdling shrieks. A peppering of plumbatae flew past her as she dodged even the best throws.

His men looked questioningly at him. "What are you waiting for? We can't let her kill them all!" he yelled at them. Shouting as one, his men left cover and ran at their opponents.

Corbus watched Amalia launch herself into the wavering shield wall. *Mother, what are you doing?* he wondered as he ran after his men. The dark red *scuta* shook with the force of her blows as her spear twirled and twisted in seemingly unnatural ways. Several men went down, their comrades dragging them out of the line of battle. *Do you have a death wish?*

~ * * * ~

The sudden arrival of a second enemy force threw the somewhat jubilant post-battle celebrations into chaos as Julius bellowed, "*Form shield wall!*" He turned, pushing men toward the opponents. "Remember your training! Keep your body low and lock your shields together!"

No sooner had he given the order than a flight of crossbow bolts neatly eviscerated a chunk of his own force. One bounced off of Julius's helmet. Stars floated before his eyes before he shook them off. *We must get into formation, or we will all die!* part of his brain screamed at him as he fought furiously to work some moisture into his dry mouth.

Julius drew his sword. Their training had engraved in every legionnaire's mind that it was not smart or proper to go about waving your sword over your head in a combat situation. That was not the Roman style. *Screw the Roman style. Desperate times call for desperate measures.* He leapt atop a crenellation; whirling his sword in the air and calling for his men to rally, *rally* to me! For a few brief moments, the line steadied, men moving shoulder to shoulder, ranks forming as they should behind them. The roughly thirty remaining men of his command clumped together across the walkway.

Julius spotted Legionnaire Faustus crouched to one side, cursing as he attempted to tie a strip of cloth around his bleeding shield arm. "Faustus! Get back and find the tribune. Tell him we need assistance immediately! The rebels are making a break for it!" The man gave a sketchy salute and sprinted along the walkway, hand gripping the cloth over his bleeding forearm.

A thin, piercing howl reached his ears and worked its way down his spine into his belly. Knees trembling, he covered his ears with his hands and felt a wetness against his palms. His men were doing the same, several falling to their knees, dropping their shields and plumbatae in the effort to escape the ear-rending noise. "Keep together, men!" Julius tried to cry out, but it came out as a mere croak.

A woman was moving rapidly toward their line, and the sound seemed to move in response to her movements. His mind garbled frantically at him, as his spirit fought to remain strong against the overwhelming horror of the shrieking, *It's like one of the furies come to life.* He noticed her weapon: a long, dark metallic shaft capped on either end with a wicked-looking sickle-shaped blade. *That's something out of a bad theater production, only I bet that blade isn't made of scrap metal.*

He screamed, trying to overwhelm her punishing, unceasing psychological attack. Putting every ounce of command authority he had into his voice, Julius dug deep down into his soul and cried out one last time, trying desperately to gather his soldiers. "*Hold,* fellow Romans, HOLD THE LINE!"

He straightened, and began grabbing cloaks and collars, pulling at his men with a strength born from the fires of desperation and fear. He shoved a few into the weak battle line, and the men gained strength from their companions. Gwendyrn, blood dripping down his mustache and onto his beard from his nose and ears, grabbed two men with his meaty hands and heaved them to their feet. He roughly shoved discarded weapons at them. The men turned toward the front line, Gwendyrn close behind, forming an unstoppable bulwark against terror.

The fury-like creature rushing their thin, red line choose that moment to strike. Julius's mouth dropped open as she *leapt* three ranks of men, landing behind the shield wall, in the midst of the shaken defenses. Her spear sliced out, wounding and incapacitating men. Julius turned toward another yell from beyond the wall to see the remaining rebel fighters charging. The demi-cohort was trapped between a mob of attackers on one side, and a crazed death-dealer on the other.

Mind racing, Julius considered his options. He could try to push past the crazed Amazon behind them, or charge the rebels in front of them. *On one side we lose to ferocity and skill, on the other we lose to numbers.* Julius did the only thing he could think of. "Form square!" he ordered.

His men moved into position, forming a tight square with the crenellated wall as the fourth side of the formation. The sides formed by the men were spiked with plumbatae and swords. Stragglers crawled toward them, while others limped into position just before the shields closed over them. Julius listened to the heavy panting of his men as they struggled to catch their breath before the inevitable onslaught, and heard Gwendyrn whispering prayers to Jupiter above to save them. "Didn't know you were a praying man," he quipped.

Gwendyrn paused and looked down at him. "I just figure now's as good a time as any to start."

Julius considered this, then partially closed his eyes and muttered an abbreviated prayer to Minerva, his patron goddess. *Please, let us get rescued; I don't want to die.* It might have been selfish, it might have been self-serving, but he didn't want to die on this black steel wall at the age of twenty. *Somebody help us!*

~ * * * ~

Seeing the remaining legionnaires forming a square flush with the wall at their backs, Corbus ordered his men to halt their charge and form ranks. His mother paced back and forth, occasionally letting loose another heart-tearing scream.

Corbus coolly analyzed the situation. Although shaken, the Roman remnants would not go down easily. Those big shields and their tight training would translate to many casualties among his more lightly armored men.

He was still seeking a competent decision when the faint whir of an airship's engines reached him. He cocked his head, trying to drown out the sounds of the wounded and dying men nearby, and the sea far below. A gust of wind pushed the clouds farther out, unveiling the prow of a gray airship, slicing through the last clouds toward the platform.

"Remain here; keep those sheep penned in," he called to Fustus, his newly-appointed subordinate.

The man's lips curled in a tight smile and he sent the men to spread out facing the beleaguered remnants of the Roman cohort and pepper the formation with heavy repeater darts, trying to find a weak spot in the formation.

Corbus's boots crunched over the film of dried sea salt and sand that had built up along the wall top. Years of salt and rain had done surprisingly little damage to the wall, but with the recent conflict, the maintenance men hadn't reached this stretch to clean it and reseal it. He peered up at the floating ship as it grew larger and larger. Finally able to make out the engine design, he smiled. It was the *Midgard Flyer*. He waved at the cockpit and someone on the bridge waved in return. The airship continued its ponderous progress, rising slightly as it came over the low lip of the landing pad. Already he could see a hatch opening along its gray-painted side, revealing a dark but nonetheless inviting interior.

Turning, Corbus called out to his men, "Fall back to the landing pad. It's high time we left this den of corruption! Let our retribution be felt for an age." He sneered at the Romans cowering within their shielded formation. *It won't matter how protected they think they are. Soon this whole city shall deal with the wrath of our movement, our peoples. Deus Ex Mortalitas!*

"But why do I have to come with you?" came a whine from the small huddle of civilians the rebels had brought with them. Chalbys had been among that lucky group. "Wouldn't it make more sense for me to remain here, providing you with information and passing instructions to our followers?"

Corbus frowned. He disliked the monocle-eyed, sniveling, luxury-loving spymaster, and everything he represented. "My mother seems to believe that the *cause* would be better served by having you join us." He waved a hand toward the remaining rebels, now cautiously backing away toward the ship. "Besides, every truly loyal rebel is here with us, now. We just staged an insurrection, and if those loyalists have any brains, which *this* commander does, they will be looking for anyone with a connection to the rebellion. So it would really be foolish to leave a valuable person like you behind." He smiled condescendingly. *You cowardly wimp.* Seemingly resigned to his fate, Chalbys sighed, and trudged toward the airship with the rest of the civilians.

With a soft crunch and bump, the *Midgard Flyer* touched down behind them. Several air marines stepped out, slim crossbows and short swords held at the ready. They fanned out to cover the remaining rebels as they retreated toward the ship. Corbus smiled. They were getting out of this forsaken place. There was nothing here for them anymore. And soon, there would be nothing left here for anyone, anymore.

Many of his men were boarding the airship when disaster struck.

A battle cry rose beyond the isolated Roman detachment, heralding the entrance of a new opponent: a new batch of Roman legionnaires, racing along the wall, weapons at the ready.

Amalia had not retreated toward the ship when the call had come, remaining instead at her position on the wall. She stood rooted by surprise for a moment, then lifted her weapon, and the dance of death began in earnest.

Chalbys and Fustus cried out in alarm at the legionnaires' arrival. The situation had rapidly changed from one of playfully toying with the surrounded Roman detachment to being suddenly outnumbered. With most of their men embarked, there were few men left to help their leader. The air marines' cordon was shrinking as they hastily converged on their only escape, leaving the three ringleaders out in the open.

Chalbys glanced at Fustus. "All is lost, but we cannot allow her to fall," Chalbys offered. Fustus looked worried, his face etched with lines of concentration. They looked at Corbus.

Hard pressed to hold back the overwhelming tide of the legionary force, Amalia was a blur whose touch left injury and death. Then, mobbed by at least ten different legionnaires, she went down. Those on the landing platform about fifty yards away heard her cry out. With an involuntary gasp, Corbus stepped forward, only to see his mother's opponents flying in all directions. One hurtled off the wall into open space, plummeting toward the city below. She fought to stand again, heavily favoring her right side.

Corbus pulled his swords out, but both of the other men were one step ahead of him. For the first time in his life, Corbus felt himself being manhandled, each man grasping an arm as they fought to prevent him from the suicide of charging into the enemy ranks. Despite Chalbys's weak appearance, his grip was like an iron vise.

"We ... can't ... lose ... you ... too. We'd have lost everything for no gain!" gasped Fustus as they wrestled the frantic assassin toward the safety of the ship.

As he fought to go to the aid of his mother, Corbus saw the remnants of the original Roman detachment finally regain their nerve and advance on the airship, moving in good order. The last few air marines stood nearby, one firing his crossbow at the legionnaires who had managed to get around Amalia's human blockade. The man let out a scream as he fell, attracting more attention to the grounded ship. The Romans were getting closer, their feet pounding on the parapet.

"We can't stay here, sir! You'll just die like your mother," Fustus growled.

Over the man's shoulder, Corbus watched Amalia fighting like a cornered tiger. His face felt wet, and he realized he was

Hard pressed to hold back the overwhelming tide of the legionary force, Amalia was a blur whose touch left injury and death.

crying. His so-called allies were dragging him away from helping his *mother*, the only family member he had even known. "Come on, Mother!" he screamed, trying desperately to get her to leave with them.

Amalia turned to look at him. For a moment, their eyes connected, and Corbus felt as though a huge weight had been transferred to his shoulders. Her eyes were full of love and zeal, full of anger and protectiveness. With that last glance, she turned to continue her defense, backing slowly toward the landing pad while keeping as many Imperials as busy as possible.

Chalbys and Fustus bundled Corbus onto the relative safety of the airship. Behind them, the last marine leapt onto the deck and rang a bell. The tone of the ship's engines changed as it went buoyant and began gaining altitude.

Below them, the Romans who had nearly reached them threw a volley of plumbatae at the rapidly retreating ship, but most of the metal bolts clanked off the bottom of the decking. One came close enough for Corbus to hear its passage before it rebounded off a nearby post and back into space, its warhead fizzling without exploding.

Chalbys and Fustus remained beside Corbus as he stood on the deck, regardless of the assurances he had given them that he no longer wished to take on half the Roman army single-handed. All he could do now was watch as the Romans surrounded and overwhelmed his mother. His heart felt as though it was being ripped out of his chest.

The figures on the landing platform shrank as the *Midgard Flyer* gained altitude. Claxons began to wail. Corbus was dimly aware of another airship approaching. His full attention remained on the fight. It was as if he was watching a tragic drama from the cheap seats; heart pounding, the young man could do nothing but watch and see what happened as the red-coated figures surrounded the brown-coated one.

~ * * * ~

"Move forward! Quickly—we've got to reach that landing platform and destroy that airship!" Constantine ordered.

His men continued to push against the solitary figure guarding the walkway. While they had managed to relieve the pressure on the small knot of surviving legionnaires, they had been unable to move past the rebel Amazon. Behind her, Constantine could see that Centurion Caesar had reestablished command and was moving to intercept the airship.

Constantine pushed through the ranks of his men. They were hanging back, having seen the damage the woman's double-ended spear could do, even to an armored man. Constantine's feet slipped in blood and gore. At one point he was fairly certain that he had stepped upon a dead soldier, his arm sliced off. As he stepped into the front ranks, he lurched as his foot found another slick spot on the causeway. The stumble saved his life—the twirling figure's steel sliced right over his helmet, chopping off his officer's plume, the force of the glancing blow snapping the chinstrap on his helmet to rip it right off his head.

Constantine sucked in a shaky breath, and exhaled in a gasp as he pulled his shield up in time to deflect another blow. *I need to maneuver more!* His memories of private dueling and combat instruction clamored to be used. Yet he was shoulder to shoulder with his men, unable to truly maneuver other than forward or backward. Forward it was. There was no going back.

The ranks pressed forward under his shouted orders. The open space of the landing platform was less than ten yards away now. Taking a quick peek over his shield, Constantine saw that most of the enemy had boarded. A few men appeared to be watching the conflict with extreme interest. As the legionnaires advanced, two of the men grasped a third and began hauling him back to the ship, as crewmembers on the ship fired crossbows, dealing light damage as they harried the Imperial attack.

The woman's spear shattered the metal-wood composite shield of the man beside Constantine and thrust into his organs, killing him horribly in a split second. Seeing an opening, Constantine took it, stabbing out with his spatha and cutting her leg. *A solid hit; Duel Master Vusentius would be proud,* he thought as his sword came back with blood on the blade.

Screaming in pain, the woman backed off a few steps to recover from the obviously painful wound. The startled legionnaires followed cautiously. As they chased her, the fire from the dirigible became more accurate. One legionnaire's startled yell was quickly silenced as another crossbow bolt ripped out part of his neck.

Straining, the airship lifted off, unwilling to allow the Imperials to get too close. Centurion Caesar 's detachment peppered them with plumbata, even though the light missiles had little chance of harming such a vessel. The plain warheads sounded like rain on a tin roof as they bounced off the iron deck plating.

The devilish woman finally turned in the middle of the landing platform to face her pursuers. Hatred burned in her eyes as she stared down the dozens of men surrounding her.

Constantine looked around. "Julos! Get some men on those anti-airship weapons! I want that ship taken down, *now!*" he ordered. A squad peeled off and ran toward the large anti-air scorpions and ballistae.

Shrieking her defiance, the woman charged at *him. Guess that order upset her,* his mind observed as he raised his shield and leapt forward to attack.

His men formed a circle around the pair, shields facing in. They knew that Constantine was a solid warrior, but could he compare to this queen of death? They began to bang the flat of their blades against their scuta, inching closer, tightening the ring around Constantine and their opponent. Trapped, the Amazon grasped her spear tightly, and launched a rapid assault.

Constantine felt his reflexes speed up; he *saw* her attacks coming. His blade moved almost before he commanded it to as he parried high, then low, then slammed his shield forward, knocking her off balance. She skipped back out of range again, her scythe-like speartip pushing back the encroaching ranks of legionnaires as it cracked shields and sliced open arms.

She's stalling for time. That airship, or someone on it, must be critical to her, for her to make a last stand defense. He paused in his attack, and heard no heavy artillery being fired. With a sinking feeling, he raised his voice. "Centurion! Why is there no artillery firing?"

Centurion Caesar pushed to the edge of the circle. His armor was heavily banged up and he had several superficial wounds. "Sir!" he croaked. "All the artillery pieces have been sabotaged or destroyed. There's no way for us to shoot it down from here. Klotus evidently managed to contact the *Scioparto* via the tower line, and it's already moving to intercept."

The woman cast a look of such venom at Julius that he took a step back. She spoke for the first time. "I am Brimmas Amalia, Chieftess of the warrior tribes of the Teutonberg. My ancestors fought yours and killed many a Roman weakling. It is my pleasure to bring you all into the afterlife with me, Tribune." Her mouth stretched in an evil smile as she prepared herself.

Constantine considered her words. "After you," he replied.

Closing the space between them in an instant, they clashed again. Constantine got inside her guard, breaking her spear with a well-timed smash of his heavy scuta. *Yes!* his mind cried as he heard it snap, then her brief cry of despair. But the woman was crafty. She quickly disarmed Constantine with a sharp blow to his sword hand, using the broken haft of her weapon as a club.

His hand stung and he was fairly certain that he had felt something go *pop.* A tendon perhaps, or maybe a bone was broken. He turned in time to catch the next attack on his shield. Amalia now wielded one piece of her broken weapon like a short stabbing spear, thrusting it out at Constantine as they circled each other, no doubt hoping the hooked end would catch the lip of his shield and yank it from his possession.

From far overhead came the thrum of airship engines. The Romans cheered as the H.M.A.S. *Scioparto* shifted to engage the slow-moving *Midgard Flyer.*

"Looks like your friends won't be getting away after all. You've sacrificed yourself for nothing," Constantine jeered in his most arrogant, imperial tone. Out of the corner of his eye, he saw that Julius had drawn his sword and had nudged his neighbors farther away from him.

"You'll make good company in Hades, foolish Imperial. Prepare to die." With that, Amalia threw herself forward again. Her first blow knocked Constantine's shield aside and he felt it torn from his arm as he rolled to the left.

"Centurion! Sword!" he shouted.

Julius tossed him his sword, the deadly spatha turning in the air; Constantine caught its haft with his left hand and turned to face the chieftess, who was disentangling her weapon from the scuta.

She smiled coldly, no doubt thinking that he was weakened, now that he was forced to use his left hand. She rushed in and knocked at his sword with less effort than he expected. *Her mistake—but then, how could she know that Master Vusentius required all his pupils to learn to fight with both hands?* He easily turned the blow away and dropped into a neat central slice.

He looked up from one knee to see his handiwork. Amalia stumbled, looked down at the deep red gash that cut across her stomach, then fell backward.

Constantine rose. As his men rushed in to congratulate him, he held up his hand to stop their inquiries and exultations, and kicked away her weapons. Then he knelt by her side.

Her bloodstained lips twisted in a grimace. Then she worked her mouth for a moment and spat bloodied spittle in his face. "See you soon," she croaked.

He stood and looked around. "What could that mean?" he wondered aloud.

Then he felt a gentle tremor, which grew to a shake, and then a roar as the wall beneath his feet *lifted* him off the ground. Farther to the south, parts of the wall were being launched into the city and the bay by a powerful blast. Huge columns of dirty gray water erupted from the wall and rushed to fill the city. Thick smoke rose into the sky, following rocketing debris.

"Quick! Into the tower!" someone yelled, and the men raced toward the safety of the guard towers, rocks and water and sizzling hot fragments falling all around them. A particularly huge chunk of wall hurtled toward them and slammed into the walkway like a freight train. Constantine was thrown off his feet, and darkness took him.

EPILOGUE

FROM HIS BED IN THE governor's lavish mansion, a convalescing Constantine stared up at the white mesh fabric draped over the bed at ceiling level, forming a translucent pavilion around his bed. Snapping to his senses, he sat up abruptly, then stopped just as abruptly as his stomach twisted, protesting such quick movement. He dropped sideways and was thankful to see a wastebin beside the bed as his breakfast made a U-turn in his gut.

Several minutes later, he wiped his mouth and rolled back from the wastebin to carefully sit up. Pushing aside the gauze curtain, he swung his legs over the side of the bed and gingerly got to his feet, curiosity driving him to examine his hospital ward. He knew he'd been here for a week. He'd lost all memory of the events on the wall after this close combat duel with the warrior chieftess, Amalia, and had relied on visitors' accounts to refresh it.

He'd not been wearing his helmet when the explosion came, leaving his head unprotected during the aerial deluge produced by the massive explosion that ruptured the sea wall. Engineers examining the aftermath estimated that the explosives needed to rupture the sixty-foot thickness of the steel and stone wall must have been stored in a warehouse that touched the wall, and that the rebels had likely been drilling into the wall for months to place the explosives at its true center, already weakening it from the inside out—all part of a nefarious plot to destroy the very city the rebels had fought so hard to seize.

"They might even have used acids or seawater on a targeted portion of the wall to weaken it. That would have taken weeks of planning, if not months," one engineer had reported to him. That spoke of better planning and treason that ran much deeper than what anyone had suspected.

Within seconds of the explosion, the Mar del Nort had come flooding into the city, wiping out the low-lying Sludge Bottom and reaching as far as the heavily damaged air terminal in the northern quadrant and the central plaza in the eastern part. Estimates of dead or missing were in the tens of thousands. Between the flood and the fighting, most of the city garrison and constabulary auxilia were dead or injured. The XIII Germania had become the enforcers of martial law until fresh auxilia forces arriving from the south and east could relieve them.

Two figures approached Constantine as he turned back toward his bed. He smiled as Centurion Julius Caesar raised a hand in greeting; he *should* be smiling, Constantine thought, now that Legion Command Northwest had confirmed word of his brevet rank of centurion. Unfortunately the confirmation of rank had dumped weeks of overdue paperwork onto the newly minted centurion's shoulders, as well. Constantine didn't envy the young man that.

Maria, the head nurse, scuttled behind the centurion, already fluttering her hands in agitation. The appearance of the junior officer always left Constantine in, as she put it, an especially challenging mood. Like many nurses, she considered her word to be law. Her patient *would* rest the proper amount of time prescribed by the doctors, or *else.*

Julius was walking much faster than normal. Constantine knew that he did not like to disturb the men recuperating in the ranks of beds that stretched along the wall on either side of Constantine's. Today, though, his boots click-click-clicked across the floor, forcing Maria, shorter by a head and a half, to nearly run to keep up.

"You will not disturb my peace and quiet during non-visiting hours!" he heard her saying as they drew nearer.

Constantine placed his hand on the bed frame to help alleviate a brief moment of dizziness. *I must have taken a fairly substantial knock on the head,* he thought for the umpteenth time. *At least I didn't lose all of my memory, as some men do. Imagine having to be taught how to be a legionnaire for a* second *time!*

He held up his hand to stop the nurse. "Now, Maria," he said in a mollifying voice. "I'm sure that the centurion here had a good reason for interrupting your perfectly good midday nap." He smiled his best smile.

Flustered, the nurse backed away. She checked the large clock on the wall at the end of the ward. "Five minutes, then you're out of here, regardless of how 'important' that paper is." She waggled a finger at the pouch Julius's waist, scowling, then turned and stomped back out of the ward. Constantine cringed. Julius looked apologetic.

When the door punctuated Maria's exit from the ward, Constantine observed, "That is one woman I would not like to be on the wrong side of." He looked at Julius. "And yet I get the feeling I'll still be suffering for your little invasion later tonight, when I get poked and prodded with needles at two a.m. What is so important that you broke multiple layers of rules and actually penetrated our vast and uncaring medical bureaucracy?"

He was truly curious. In the short time he had known Julius as an officer, he had pegged him as a by-the-books centurion, especially since he hadn't yet learned all the ins and outs of working the system. *Not that I've been able to yet, but all I have to do is wave my Imperio signet coin in the air and it parts the sea like magic.*

Julius displayed a face-splitting grin. He leaned closer to the tribune to whisper conspiratorially, "We've got orders."

Constantine smiled as well, although it became a tad frozen by another short bout of dizziness. It had been happening less and less, thank the gods, but still often enough to really annoy him. "Excellent. I'll be glad to get out of this hellhole." At Julius's stricken expression, he quirked an eyebrow. "What, Centurion? Just because it used to be a grand metropolis doesn't mean it's that way anymore. Maybe in a few years it will be again, when they've rebuilt the wall and purged the flooded areas. Until then, this city is a hellhole. A toxic, disease-ridden, soggy, smelly, and somehow still functioning, hellhole. We need to get out of here."

Julius sighed. "I suppose so, sir," he mumbled.

Constantine remembered the root of Julius's sadness. "Have you found any trace of your family yet?" he asked in a softer voice.

Julius shook his head. "I borrowed a few squads to comb the neighborhood. I found some things of theirs, but there were no bodies or survivors. I can't tell if the destruction is from the explosion, the fighting, or the flood." He spread his hands in frustration. "I'm not giving up hope, though. I can feel they are alive." His voice hardened. "I want to deliver some painful vengeance on those who did this."

Constantine nodded. "Don't give up hope. Besides, there is always retribution, as well." Both men grinned. "So, are you going to tell me those orders, before Nurse-Empress Maria comes marching her way back into the ward to throw you out on your behind?"

Julius reached into his belt pouch and withdrew the sheaf of orders. He handed them over to the tribune. Constantine read them over, while Julius tried hard not to look as if he was attempting to read through the thin parchment.

Constantine rolled up the orders and handed them back to the centurion. "Well, Centurion, before you go, I have a question." Julius tried to hide his disappointment that the tribune was not going to share their orders. Constantine smiled. "Have you requisitioned your cold weather gear yet? 'Cause I think it's about time we taught those fur-coated northern barbarian raiders a lesson: Don't. Mess. With. Us."

The End

TERMINOLOGY

Cohort – a company of Roman legionnaires. Cohorts from different legions tend to vary in size, with newly formed legions having the most consistent cohort size. In each legion there can be as many as thirty cohorts, with the first, or Prime, cohort being the most veteran, most talented, and composed of the most dangerous fighters in the entire legion.

Demi-cohort – a partial cohort, consisting of anywhere between fifty and a hundred men.

Denarius (denarii, plural) – the base unit of Roman money, roughly equivalent to a dollar.

Galea – a Type L Imperial Italic Roman steel helmet with side cheek pieces, banded forehead piece, neck protector, and chinstrap. Generally mass-produced, it is rugged and can withstand several years of hard campaigning with minimum upkeep. It has been continuously updated since the early Imperial era, and additional technology, such as the high altitude goggles, has been added as necessary.

Plumbata – a Roman throwing dart with a weighted metal tip. The average soldier carries several of them in the hollow of his shield. Some are tipped with an explosive warhead instead, creating a weapon similar to a grenade.

Primus Caesar, primus imperio – Used interchangeably, the terms refer to the First Caesar, or the heir to the throne of Imperial Rome. The emperor designates an heir, known as the primus caesar, who is placed above all other sons in the line of succession. Generally assigned by age, precedence has been altered during the reign of some emperors due to scandal, treachery, assassination, or simple favoritism. The term secondus, or tercius is used to when referring to the second or third in line from the throne.

Scuta – a Roman shield with central metal boss and rounded rectangular shape. The shield is slightly concave to better protect the bearer from missiles and blows.

Spatha – the next advancement of the original gladius sword adapted from the Iberian tribes. Similar in design, but with an extra two feet of reach, the spatha provides heavier hitting power for modern-day legionnaires.

Made in the USA
San Bernardino, CA
01 April 2013